Midnight Love

A Novel By

Kella

Midnight Love

Copyright © 2021 by Marquel Amos

Acknowledgements

To my dear friend K.C., thank you for pushing me to complete my book. Since high school, you have been a fan of my writing and creativity. I thank you for always holding me accountable and making sure that I executed my childhood dream.

Chapter 1

Tiffany-Montgomery, AL

December 2016

"Come on, baby!! We only have a few seconds before you go into this meeting. Let me check your tie and collar." I checked my husband for any last-minute mistakes that he could have made due to being anxious and nervous. I took out my chap stick and put some on his lips. He had been biting them for the past 10 minutes, and now they were all dried out.

"Okay, you're all set. Now we sit and wait. And don't touch those lips again. Don't want to go in there with crusty lips, do you?"

Calvin smirked and shook his head no.

We sat outside of his boss' office waiting for him to be called in. I could tell he was extremely nervous. His hands were shaky, and he had sweat building on his forehead. I dabbed his forehead with a napkin from my purse and eased my hand into his. I tried to ease his mind by giving him a brief pep talk and some words of encouragement.

"Baby, you got this. You are the top anchor in all of Montgomery. Houston will be happy to have you. Don't worry, honey." I kissed his hand, which was shaking and sweaty.

"This is why I love you. You always know what to say. You are my number one supporter, Tiffany."

"After 12 years of being together, and 5 years of marriage. You better love me!" We laughed at my smart remark.

A few minutes passed by and his boss walked out of his office. He called out to Calvin.

"Mr. Willow, I am ready to see you now."

His boss stood in the doorway, and waited for Calvin to walk in. I smiled and waved at his boss. He nodded and smiled in return. Calvin then disappeared into his boss' office.

I waited with anticipation. Since no one else was on this floor, I could let out all my nervous emotions. I had been trying to be strong in front of Calvin; but hell, I was just as nervous as he was! I was nervous about the reality of moving to Houston, Texas. I would be moving away from all my family and friends. I didn't even move away for college, because I was so attached to my family.

Another thing I was nervous about was resigning from

my job. I am currently a communications engineer for Alabama State University's sports department. But with the money he is going to be making in Houston, he told me I wouldn't have to work anymore. I have always had job security since I started working in ASU's communications department my Junior Year of college. All of this was going to be different for me. It was a step out on faith. It would be a new journey, but I was willing to walk this road. I will always support my husband, and I trust that he is making the best decision for us.

I snapped out of my feelings when I heard the doorknob turn. After what felt like an eternity, Calvin finally emerged from his boss' office. He walked smoothly over to me, but he couldn't hold his excitement any longer.

"I got it baby!!! Out of all the candidates that applied, I got it!!!!" He said as he oozed with excitement.

I opened my arms as wide as I could; embracing him with the biggest hug I could give. I then kissed his lips over and over. I caught a glimpse of his boss. He smiled and gave me a thumbs-up. I returned his thumbs up.

"See, I told you honey. All those other applicants didn't stand a chance against Calvin Willow!!!! My Calvin Willow!! I'm proud of you honey, let's celebrate!"

We left the building and walked to the car; both smiling like children who just opened their Christmas presents. The presents that you really wanted and fantasized about playing with all year.

We went to the Alley BAR in downtown Montgomery and ordered our usual drinks to start this celebration off right. We then looked at the televisions that were mounted on the walls. One of them had Calvin's news station on.

"Look, Calvin. Get a good look at that set. Your handsome face will no longer appear on it. Next time the world sees you, PXBN will be at the bottom of the screen."

Calvin smiled and nodded his head in agreement.

We drank and watched as crimes, weather, sports, fire rescues, and an older black couple who were celebrating 75 years of marriage were covered.

"So, what did your boss say? How'd he break it down to you?"

Calvin sipped his Grand Marnier real slow, keeping me in suspense.

"Well, he basically said that my tape was better than all the other applicants. I connected more and seemed to engage more with the other staff. All that running back and forth to the Houston news station worked in my favor, and that the Houston crew were very pleased with my diligence. Only thing is, and I was afraid to tell you this, but the position starts in a month."

Wow! A month was shorter than I expected. I instantly thought about how I was going to tell my family that I was moving to another city and state within the next month.

Calvin continued on.

"My boss said that the station is going to provide us with a home for a year; fully furnished. And after that, we would have to financially provide our own place. So, I figured since you won't be working; you can take care of that and find us a home by that time frame ends."

"Sure honey. You just worry about doing well. What area would we be moving into in Houston? I want to look it up on Google and do my investigation."

"The area is called Missouri City. It's a suburb city outside of the Southwest area of Houston. Our neighborhood will be Sienna Plantation."

"Ok, I'll get on it." Our food soon arrived, and we both dug into or meals. Both of us were so nervous about his meeting today, we skipped lunch.

After eating, we headed back home. We opened the door and was greeted with both of our families and friends.

"Surprise!" They all yelled out as we entered the home and cut the lights on.

I planned a surprise party for Calvin because I already knew he was going to get the job. I could just feel it; call it 'Wife's Intuition'.

Genuinely surprised, he turned and blushed at me.

"Thank you, baby!" He said to me before kissing me on

the lips.

"You're welcome. You deserve it. You worked so hard and got the promotion! I'm proud of you baby." I said before kissing him again.

I then walked away and left him to mingle with everyone. I made my way to the kitchen to start feeding our guests. My sister soon walked up behind me. It wasn't long before she started talking her shit.

"I hope this nice gesture gets him to appreciate you. *You really outdid yourself this time, Tiffany.* Maybe it'll be the push he needs to open his goddamn eyes!"

I rolled my eyes.

"Tracy, please don't start that shit with me! Goddamn, I just got in the house. What about a hi Tiffany, how are you doing? Or a simple hello? Can we start there?"

My sister Tracy. Can't live with her, couldn't live without her. Tracy and I have a very combative relationship. But I love her, nonetheless. You can't choose family. Just have to learn to love them.

She continued.

"I *started* by helping you plan this party. I *started* by cooking majority of the food, decorating, and getting everyone over here for your trifling ass husband. And did I receive a thank you? No, I did not."

"You didn't even give me a chance to say thank you. You

came over here messing with me as soon as I got through the door!" We stared at each other; both looking like we wanted to slap each other. My mother then walked in.

"Hey, hey, hey. You two stop all that. Been fighting since you were kids. Not tonight. Tracy, show your little sister some respect in her house."

My mother then hugged and kissed me and walked off. I then poked my tongue out at Tracy.

"I don't give a damn what mama said. I want to hear it. Say it. Say, thank you Tracy."

"Thank you. *Bitch.*"

We both laughed and hugged each other.

"You're welcome, *bitch*. Now see, was it that hard?"

I rolled my eyes as my response.

It was no secret that Tracy and Calvin didn't get along. Hopefully, they could make it work until the time we left for Houston next month. Which, I was afraid to tell Tracy. I was planning to take it one step at a time. I didn't want an episode to go down like last Thanksgiving. Things got so bad that holiday; I thought they could never be in a room together again. But fortunately, they are better. Baby steps.

I left Tracy in the kitchen and went back out to the party.

I must admit, Tracy has her reasons for feeling the way she does about Calvin. Calvin has cheated on me quite a few times before. Last year right after Labor Day, Calvin was caught in the act cheating on me. Again. And this time, he was caught by Tracy. Of all people! Tracy physically seeing him with her own eyes was the worst possible thing! She already couldn't stand him from the previous times he's cheated and hurt me. And listening to all of my tears and sob stories also didn't help when I decided to take him back each time. I can't fault her for looking out for her little sister.

I'll never forget how it went down.

Tracy was out celebrating with some friends and saw Calvin and the other woman at a restaurant on the northside. Tracy managed to get video and pictures of them laughing, holding hands, feeding each other, kissing; the whole nine yards. The previous times he has cheated on me, I always found out because the girls texted or called me. But this one hit different. Seeing him on video enjoying himself with another woman cut me to the core. I would never get that woman's face out of mind. And an image is all I have. I never got the chance to find out her name or anything else. Tracy said when she confronted Calvin about it, the woman ran out of there so fast.

From the videos and pictures, I could see that she was a pretty woman. She also looked younger. Really younger. Honestly speaking, she looked like a black Barbie doll. Very polished, and well put together. Made me insecure, made me feel basic, made me feel like my husband wanted more out of a woman. I also wondered if that's the reason he kept cheating on me. Maybe I let myself go over these past years.

But, since then, I've been working on my image. Trying to spruce myself up a bit and win my husband's attraction back to me.

As much as I was going to miss my family, this was one of the reasons why I was excited to get out of Alabama. I wanted to be somewhere fresh and new. Away from all the judgement I received for staying with Calvin. I know my parents didn't judge me, but I hated disappointing them. Especially my daddy. I hated crying in his arms then going right back to Calvin. As much as he wanted to be supportive; I know he disliked Calvin for how he made his baby girl feel. But most of all, Tracy. She was always making me feel bad for the decisions I've made. And as the younger sister, I always wanted to please her.

I've been with Calvin since I was 16 years old; a junior in high school. He's the only man I've ever been with. I didn't know any different. We have had our ups and downs over the years, but what couple hasn't? We've been through marriage counseling and got past our issues. I'm putting my trust and faith in our marriage. God will see us through. I just hope that one day, things would get better and we could all be one big happy family. I think a little distance between my family and Calvin would do us some good. Out of sight, out of mind.

Maybe my family will forget and forgive the things Calvin has done; once he's not in their faces all the time.

I shook those feelings and got my head back in what was going on right now. I walked over to the serving tables where I joined my mother and Tracy in making plates for the guests.

Chapter 2

D. Glove-Houston, TX

December 2016

It was Saturday night, 6pm. I was on my way to pick up my brother Daniel and his wife Jalisa. We were going to my partner in crime's farewell dinner party at Eddie V's. Mr. Thomas was my engineer for my radio show: Midnight Love. He was my right-hand man for the past 10 years. He taught me everything when I first came into this radio media business. I'm still in shock that he's leaving the station. But he has been with the company since it started over 30 years ago. I'm pretty sure he's ready for retirement. I could understand that it's time to move on. At least I had him with me until Christmas.

I arrived at my brother's home. He and Jalisa came out and walked to my car. They got in, and we headed to the party. As soon as she could, Jalisa started grilling me about my love life.

"Think we might meet your soul mate, or your sheets mate tonight at the party?"

Before I even had a chance to answer, Daniel answered for me.

"His sheets mate. This boy ain't ready to settle down yet!"

And he was right. I fist bumped him as we laughed.

"My big brother knows me all too well. There are too many women out here just to have one. Granted, I'm happy for you both. But for me? Nah. It ain't happening, captain. You just got to accept me being y'all third wheel Jalisa."

Daniel and Jalisa were one of my favorite couples, right under our parents. But as much as I loved seeing their love; I just couldn't get with the idea of being stuck with one woman.

"One day, Darryl. She's going to find you, one day. Love is going to sneak up on you and bite you in the ass. But I'll be right there to stitch you up, little brother."

Jalisa joked. I laughed.

"Hold off on the stitches Doctor Jalisa. You won't ever need those."

We arrived at Eddie V's in the Shops at River Oaks. I gave my keys to the Valet and we headed inside. We went to the banquet room where the party was. I greeted Mr. Thomas with a hug, and Mrs. Thomas with a hug and a kiss on the cheek.

"Hey, now Young Buck! I'm watching where you're

putting them lips!" Mr. Thomas joked.

"Hush it Hamp." Mrs. Thomas said as she embraced me.

I walked with them to their table and pulled out Mrs. Thomas' chair.

"Thanks, sweetie." She said with a smile. I smiled back at her.

I walked over to my table and sat down with Jalisa and Daniel. I watched as my coworkers and their families mixed and mingled with one another. As more people came, we ordered food and kicked off the festivities. Mr. Patterson, our boss, got our attention by clicking his fork on his glass.

"Tonight, is a great night; yet a sad one. We are losing the backbone of our station. We know Mr. Thomas has put in some long years and has done a lot for this company. He was one of the first guys here to help this company get off the ground. He has worked in almost every department; never too big to do anything requested of him. But where he was most loved was in that booth. Always a smile on his face to cheer us up when we came in from having a bad day. He has earned his stripes with this company, and now it is his time to relax. We will miss you, but we know it's time. Ladies and gentlemen, let's give it up for Mr. Hampton Thomas."

Everyone clapped as he stood up to speak.

"Oh, no. No need for clapping. Please, you're making me blush."

We all stopped clapping, and you could hear light giggles around the room. He continued on.

"Working for FXLV: The Groove 96.2 has been a great ride. We have done some great things for the Greater Houston community. Over these last 37 years, this station has been the only station to withstand trying times. Giving Houston the greatest R&B Hits; old and new school. The only station I will ever be proud to work for. We have raised up two accompanying stations, giving Houston even more music. I couldn't be prouder. I have met some wonderful people, and I hope I have been wonderful to each and every one of you. I thank you all for thinking this much of me; to give me this retirement party. Now let's eat before y'all change your mind and make me pay for this food. God knows I can't afford fancy places like this!! Thank you everyone!"

Everyone laughed and clapped as he finished his speech.

After we ate and drank, we all started mingling again throughout the restaurant. I went over to Mr. Thomas' table. I soaked up all the knowledge I could get, since I wouldn't be seeing him as frequently anymore.

"Stay focused in this game man. Radio and media are both a pretty competitive field. You've got to stay levelheaded. And you know what would help that?"

I already knew where he was going.

"A good woman in my corner. Yes, Mr. T. You've given

that speech a thousand times."

He shook his head and laughed at my disinterest.

"One day, she will come running along. And you will be begging for mercy. Don't say I never told you anything, Young Buck."

I looked across the bar and saw a beautiful, yet older woman staring back at me. Not too old, but I could tell she was more distinguished.

"One thing I'm begging for right now Mr. T., is to get that woman over there in my bed tonight. Excuse me, won't you?"

He smirked, "Go ahead son, don't let me stop you. I want to see how you swing that!"

I left from the table and headed over to the woman at the bar.

"Hi, baby. I'm Dar--".

She interrupted before I could even finish.

"D. Glove. I know who you are."

I smiled.

"How are you tonight, Ms.?"

"Carmen."

"How are you Ms. Carmen?"

"Better now that I've met you. I was just about to leave but couldn't until I had a conversation with you. You know, I've heard that voice many of nights on the radio. It's so much sexier now that I'm hearing it in person. And your chocolate skin is so smooth and creamy." She said as she rubbed on my arm.

I knew I had this woman in the palm of my hands. Tonight, was going to be easier than I expected.

"What's your plans when you leave here?", I asked.

"Whatever you have in mind." She replied.

And just like that, my night was set. I told Carmen to wait right there while I told my brother I was leaving. As I walked over to my brother, he had a grin on his face. Jalisa was shaking her head.

"See her? That's Carmen, my buddy for the night. Take this valet ticket, and I'll catch an Uber to your house to come get my car tomorrow morning. If she's crazy; I'll come pick it up tonight."

They shook their heads in disbelief.

"You be safe and careful, Darryl." Jalisa said.

I nodded my head at them and headed back towards Carmen. I locked eyes with Mr. T, and nodded at him as well. He raised his phone; motioning for me to check it. I looked at my phone and read a text from him.

"Can I watch?"

I laughed and looked back and him; shaking my head no. Man, I sure was going to miss his sense of humor.

I went back over to Carmen.

"I drove my brother and his wife here tonight. You wouldn't mind if I ride with you, would ya?"

"No problem. Let's roll."

I escorted Carmen out of the restaurant, and we waited outside at Valet for her car to come. A BMW 5 Series rolled up, and the guy got out and gave her the keys. She was riding pretty nice, I see.

We set off to her place and had a great conversation on the ride over. I found out she just turned 50 years old, had no kids, worked as a marketing manager, and was the oldest of three sisters. I shared with her that I was 33 years old, had an older brother, that I didn't have kids either; and she already knew what my occupation was. The drive to her house was a stretch. She lived far north of Houston, in the Woodlands. It was a pretty nice neighborhood, too. Glad I lived farther away in the Memorial area. Just in case she was crazy. My uber ride to the south side was going be high than a mofo though!

We finally made it inside, and her place was nicely decorated. I loved to see a woman that took care of her place and put thought into it. She turned on a few lights as she got settled in. I looked around at photos and paintings on the wall.

She started going up the stairs and reached out her hand for me to follow her. She didn't waste any time by leading me to her bedroom. She started kissing me and pulling at my clothes. She pushed me down on the bed. She raised her dress and stood there in a black and gold lingerie set. For a 50 year-old woman, her body was of a goddess! She lit some candles around the room. She walked to the other side of her room and came back with a tray that had two short glasses on it. She reached into her nightstand and pulled out some whiskey and a lipstick case. She placed them both on the tray. She poured me up a glass and pulled two pills out of her lipstick case. She handed one to me and told me to chase it with the whiskey. I shook my head no.

"It'll make the experience better." She said.

"I'm not into all this Carmen; I've seen too many people go downhill from this."

She laughed and shook her head.

"D. Glove, baby. I'm head of the biggest marketing company in Houston. You think I'd fuck with something that'll mess up my career? I know what I'm doing; trust me. It's just Molly. Tomorrow is Sunday, you can sleep it off."

She took hers and chased it with the whiskey. She then let her hair down and spread her legs. She started playing with herself and asked me to join her. I thought to myself, what the hell, and took the pill and chased it with whiskey. I went to her and finished what she started. She was so warm and wet. She started removing the rest of my clothes. It felt like she yanked my pants off as fast as they hit the floor. She smiled at my wood, which was standing tall. Without hesitation, she covered it with her mouth. Damn this woman felt good. I grabbed a handful of her hair and enjoyed this. She toyed with my wood and did all kinds of tricks with her tongue. I came soon after. She grabbed a towel and wiped me off. She reached into the nightstand and pulled out a condom. She put it on me and then climbed on top. She rode me like a pro!

"You feel it kicking in, baby? Let it take over."

The instant she said that, I felt the drug kick in. I flipped her over and dug in her from the back. Her ass moved like ripple waves of an earthquake. She screamed out my name as I dug into her deeper.

"Wait a minute baby, turn me over. Let me look at you."

I flipped her over and gave it to her missionary style. She gazed into my eyes.

"Deeper, baby, deeper."

I dug deeper into her. Her eyes rolled to the back of her head. I stroked her harder and faster. Then I heard those four magic words.

"I'm. About. To. Cum!"

She erupted on me, and I erupted into her. Well, inside the rubber. I laid down on top of her; both of us breathing out of control.

"Goddamn, D. That was great. I needed that after the week I had."

I rolled off her and laid on my back. She laid on top of

my chest. Soon after I heard her breathing heavier. I looked down at her, and she had drifted off to sleep. I closed my eyes and drifted off as well.

An hour later, I felt her fingers stroking me. I opened my eyes and looked at her.

"Round 2?" She asked.

"Hell yea."

Sunday Afternoon

I was awakened with the aroma of breakfast cooking in the air. I could appreciate hooking up with an older woman; they knew how to take care of a man! Fuck me and feed me; what more could I ask for? Ahh, the smell of grits, eggs, and bacon filled the room. *The holy trinity!* I got dressed and followed the aroma, which led me downstairs to the kitchen. I sat at the island, and she poured me a glass of orange juice.

"See, I told you that you would sleep it off. It's almost 3:00." She said with a smirk on her face.

I smirked back at her.

"You have a very lovely home, Carmen. I need to take some decorating tips from you."

She smiled as she fixed me a plate.

"Thanks, D. Glove."

"You can stop calling me D. Glove if you'd like. Darryl is my name."

"Okay Darryl."

She then sat down, and we ate. Food was delicious; tasted almost as good as mama's! After eating, she began clearing the table.

"What time did you plan on leaving? I have some errands to run soon with my sister."

I looked on my Uber app, and saw that the closest car was 20 minutes away.

"My car will be here in 20 minutes. I'll gather my things and will be out of your way soon."

"Sure, everything is where you left it last night."

I headed back upstairs and picked up everything I had. I checked my wallet. All of my money and credit cards were in place. I checked my pockets, and my watch and earrings were still there. I just had to be sure I didn't get played. This was the smoothest sex encounter I've had with a woman in a while. Most women were clingy after sex.

"I have extra toothbrushes in the medicine cabinet. Mouth wash and toothpaste is on the counter. Help yourself." She yelled out from downstairs.

I took care of business and went back downstairs. I looked at my app, and my ride was 2 minutes away.

"So, will I see you again, Darryl?" She asked.

"Whenever you're ready, just give me a call."

She kissed me on the lips.

"I sure will. See you soon."

I then got a call that my driver was outside.

"See you later Carmen."

I then left her home. I got into the car with my driver.

"Good afternoon, Darryl. How has your morning been so far?"

I laughed to myself.

"My morning was good. But let me tell you about last night!"

Chapter 3

Tiffany-Montgomery, AL

January 2017

It was the big day! All our things were packed and placed on the moving truck. We shipped our things off yesterday. Our cars were also shipped out yesterday. We were at the airport, waiting to board our plane. Our belongings were scheduled to arrive a few hours after we landed. Tracy was also here with us, coming to help me unpack, decorate, and get settled in. I couldn't believe I was leaving my hometown, my job, and most importantly my family. But I was ready for a change.

"All passengers, the flight from Montgomery to Houston is now boarding. Please report to Gate C." We heard over the loudspeaker.

We boarded the plane and waited for the other passengers to board. Shortly after, we took flight. Two hours later, we arrived in Houston, TX at the Bush Intercontinental Airport.

Houston looked so different from Montgomery. This was a huge airport! We followed the signs which led us to Baggage Claims. After getting our luggage, we walked to the doors and saw our driver holding a sign with 'The Willows' written on it.

"Hello all. My name is Walter from the PXBN station. I will be escorting you guys to your new home. Let me get your bags." He and another male grabbed our bags.

"Follow me."

We followed him to the truck, and he put our belongings into the trunk. He shut the door behind us. Our SUV had wine and champagne, with light refreshments. They made us feel appreciated. I think I could get used to this.

"Can you believe it baby? We are finally here! We are in Houston, TX for your new job!!" I kissed him on the lips.

"Yes baby, I am excited. I'm ready to see our new place and get settled in."

Mr. Walter chimed in.

"Excuse me Mr. Willow. The company has arranged for you to do a quick tour of the station; and then I will take you guys to your new home."

"I'm pretty sure my wife and her sister are ready to go home. Could you drop them off first? They have a lot to do inside the house."

"No baby, I want to see the station."

"Remember our belongings are arriving soon. Someone has to be there to receive it."

"You're right. We'll go home. To our *new* home." I said as I kissed him on the lips.

Before going to the house, we stopped for food. We continued on our drive and soon arrived at the house. I was pleasantly surprised. It was a newly built, one-story home, with three bedrooms and two bathrooms. The master bedroom and bathroom were closer to the front of the home. And the rest of the bedrooms and bathroom were further back of the house.

"This is a very beautiful home, Tiffany. I just wish it didn't have to be all the way out here in Texas." Tracy said.

"Well now it gives you a reason to get out of Montgomery and travel. You always said how you wanted to get out of the state of Alabama; well, here is your chance. And we have 2 extra bedrooms, so you'll always have somewhere to stay."

She hugged me.

"I just can't believe my baby sister is leaving me. I'll miss you back home."

We sat at the island in the kitchen and ate our food. After about an hour, the doorbell rang. It was the movers. We let them in and got out of their way. After a few hours of rearranging and decorating; the movers were finished. Once the movers left the home, shortly after the security system company arrived. I popped open a bottle of Cabernet wine I retrieved from our driver's car. Tracy and I finished the whole bottle while the security company installed cameras and motion detectors around the home. Sitting and talking; Tracy and I reminisced on our childhood up until now.

"I can't believe it, Tiff. You have really moved to Texas. Most of us haven't even left the state of Alabama. You're gonna make something out of this family."

I blushed at her comment.

"If you call being the wife of a news anchor making something out of the family, you have to dream bigger."

She shook her head.

"Tiffany, who helped him get to where he is? Did you forget that you were the one who got him on at ASU communications department your Junior year? That you begged your boss to give him a try when your boss declined after seeing Calvin's interview reel? That you coached him on how he could be better, teaching him different speech and engagement techniques? Tiffany, please. You deserve just as much praise as Calvin is getting. If it weren't for you; Calvin would still be struggling trying to break into media. And by the way, where is that motherfucker anyway? I know a tour don't take no damn 5 hours. Station can't be that big."

I sighed.

"Tracy, I would appreciate if you didn't talk about him like that. When are you going to put this feud between you and him behind you? I have been able to forgive him; I'm going to need you to forgive him as well."

Tracy rolled her eyes.

"I'll never be able to forgive him. To see it with my own eyes, Tiffany? I don't know how you were ever able to take him back. All that you went through, supporting him day and night; and he does that to you? And then he had the nerve to be in public when he knows he's a local celebrity. Just stupid."

"Ok, Tracy. That's enough." I said out of frustration.

But Tracy continued on as if I hadn't even said anything,

"He's still a piece of shit in my book! I hate that you are so gullible and can't see that. God, I wish you would leave his raggedy ass!"

I raised my hand for her to stop talking.

"Alright, Tracy! That's enough. I'm so sick of you! Acting like you know it all! Always running your mouth, and don't know what you're talking about! You are not married and can't keep a man to save your life! So, don't speak on how I should conduct my marriage! I'm not the one always hopping from man to man, bed to bed, dick to dick!"

That damn bottle of Cabernet was about to get me in trouble. But I have had enough of Tracy always talking down to me.

"So that's how you really feel, huh? I always knew you looked down on me because I'm the free-spirited sister.

Because I'm not dumb like you. Because I choose to be with who I want to be with, whenever I want to. Because I choose not to be committed to a man after they show their whole ass. Unlike you. Stupid bitch!"

"Well, if I'm the stupid bitch, you must be the slut bitch! Learn how to make a man stay with you after he had your pussy two or three times! Hell, you've had more men than I can count on my hands and toes! Maybe I'd be happy and free like you if I went around fucking and sucking every dick thrown at me! You call it being free spirited. I call it being a hoe!"

As soon as I said that I wish I could've taken it back. But it was too late. We were in too deep. Tracy started to tear up. I could tell that really hurt her feelings.

"You know what? I try with you. I try to move past your stupidity and judgments, but you never cease to amaze me. Fuck you and that cheating ass husband of yours. Where he at anyway? First day in Houston, and he hasn't even been to the house y'all are going to call home! We been here well over six hours! He probably found him another bitch at the station, for all we know with his trifling ass. I'm calling an Uber and getting the fuck out of here. I'll stay in a hotel until my flight back to Alabama tomorrow."

"Fine. I'm tired of your foul ass mouth, and your demeaning ways. And I'm tired of kissing your ass. You think because you're the big sister you can talk to me crazy? Hell no!"

"Talk to you crazy? Tiffany you talk to me crazy all the time! You disrespect me because I've been around the block a few times. So, don't try me with that bullshit. Get the fuck out of my way!"

Tracy started looking around and reaching for her purse. She pushed past me and bumped my shoulder really hard. I thought about smacking her ass; but went against it.

Shortly after, Calvin entered the home.

"Ladies, what's going on? The house looks great! You girls did a good job with getting everything organized."

"Yea, with no thanks to you. Where were you while we were putting up this house? It took six hours for a damn tour? Bullshit. Fuck you, Calvin! Forget both of y'all! I'm out of here!"

Tracy's phone rung with a notification and she looked down at it.

"Good, my Uber arrived just in time. Don't come crying to me when this bastard fucks over you again!"

Tracy grabbed her suitcase and left the home.

"What the hell happened in here, Tiffany?" Calvin looked puzzled.

"You happened, Calvin! *You happened!*"

"Tell me what went down, Tiff."

"Just leave me alone Calvin!" I started to choke up.

I then stormed to our bedroom and locked the door. I

sat on the bed and cried. Calvin came up to the door and knocked on it.

"Tiffany, come out or let me in please. Tell me what happened."

"I don't feel like talking right now."

Tracy and I would always get into it; but not like this. Things had gone too far this time. She had a point though. We both judged one another for our lifestyles. One of the reasons why I stayed with Calvin is because I hated the fast life she lived. And I let her know every time how I felt about the choices she's made. I called her phone, it rung once, and went to voicemail. I knew she was ignoring my call. I threw my phone on the bed and started crying again. An hour passed, and I checked her Facebook and seen she posted a status.

"This hotel is beautiful! I'm gonna hate to leave it for my flight tomorrow evening. It's been real Houston!"

Well, at least I knew she made it somewhere safely. First day in Houston, and it was already a bad one. I unlocked the door, and Calvin soon came in the room. I asked him for space, and that we would talk tomorrow. I heard him going into the bathroom and turning on the shower. After he got out, I went in and showered quickly. All of that wine and crying took a toll on me. I soon felt myself drifting off to sleep.

I woke up the next morning around 8am, with a headache. From traveling, to moving, to drinking, to fighting, to crying; I was exhausted and drained. I did not think moving would be this hard. Calvin had an early meeting at the station and was already gone from the house. I checked Tracy's Facebook and saw she was out having breakfast at a restaurant here in Houston. We were supposed to go get breakfast together. I rubbed my temples. I called her and again, it rung once then went to voicemail. I thought about leaving a voicemail or sending her a text but decided against it. She was still upset, I'm sure. I'll just keep checking her Facebook to see that she made it back home safely.

I found the nearest gym and decided to check it out and possibly sign up for a membership. I brushed my teeth, showered, got dressed, and headed out the door. I arrived at the gym. Lifetime Fitness. After checking it out and speaking with a member associate, I decided to sign up for membership. Good thing I was appropriately dressed because a Kick Boxing class was starting in 15 minutes. This would be a great way to relieve all this stress and tension I built up since last night. I found a spot and got settled in. At the beginning of class, the instructor asked if there were any first timers in the class. I reluctantly raised my hand and was welcomed by the instructor and other classmates. Since it was my first class, the instructor asked if I would come up to the front so she could keep up with me. But I declined. I didn't want too much attention on me. I just wanted to relieve some stress and go home.

After the class was over, I went up to the instructor to meet her. I didn't expect to enjoy it as much as I did. So, I felt compelled to introduce myself.

"I really enjoyed your class today. My name is Tiffany. I just moved here last night from Montgomery." I reached my hand out to shake hers.

"Oh really? I have some family that live out that way. But they're in Magnolia. You're going to love it out here in the city."

"Magnolia? No, I'm from Montgomery."

"Yea, Magnolia is in Montgomery County."

"Oh no. I'm from Montgomery, Alabama."

"Oh. Montgomery, Alabama." She laughed to herself. "Forgive me Tiffany. We have a Montgomery here too. My name is Lauren. Let me pack up my things and we can walk out together."

Lauren gathered her belongings, and we left the group room together.

"So, what brought you here all the way from Alabama?"

"My husband got a job as a news anchor on PXBN. He started today."

"That sounds like a cool job. What do you do?"

"In Alabama, I worked in sports radio as a board engineer. But now, I'm currently not working. My husband's job is enough for us right now."

"Well, aren't you living the life!"

"It feels weird to not work. But I guess that means I'll get to come to class more often and learn how to kick some ass."

I mocked a few moves that Lauren taught us in class today. She laughed at my impersonations.

"Yes, come back next class. I teach every Monday, Wednesday and Friday at 9:30AM."

"I'll be back Wednesday."

"Great. What are you doing when you leave here? I don't have another client until 3PM. Maybe I can take you to brunch and show you some of the city."

"Oh, that'll be awesome, I'd appreciate it. What do you do?"

"I'm an interior designer and stager for commercial and home properties. And of course, I teach the kick boxing class for fun and play money."

I nodded my head in agreement to having the extra cash flow.

"Maybe you can help me with adding a nice touch to our home. My sister and I did the best we could, but it could use a few additions."

"Sure, we can talk about it over brunch. Follow me out, I'm in the navy blue Benz."

I walked to my car and drove around to where she was parked. She backed out and headed to the street. I trailed her until we made it to the restaurant.

Chapter 4

D. Glove

March 2017

It has been three months, and work wasn't the same with Mr. Thomas being gone. We hired an intern engineer until we cou ld find someone more permanent. Our intern wasn't as good as Mr. Thomas, but he was getting the job done.

Despite getting adjusted to work; I've been having a good time with Carmen. She was the true definition of a friend with benefits. She was very laxed and chill. She had as much to lose in her career as I did mines. So, she kept things very casual and low profile. I liked that. I brought her around Daniel and Jalisa once; only because I was tired of being a third wheel when we go out for dinks. Daniel was cool with her, but I could tell Jalisa wasn't too comfortable with her. I know it's because she's older and a friend with benefits. Jalisa is ready for me to fall in love, and not with a cougar. Or Sugar Mama, as Jalisa likes to call it. She was ready to have a sister in law she could share these moments with. She's just going to have to be comfortable with Carmen for the time being.

Tonight wasn't about Carmen though. I had a date lined up with another chick I met while out having lunch with coworkers. Alicia. *Nurse Alicia.* I would let her take care of me any day with her fine ass. Alicia and I were meeting up at Lucille's for dinner. She insisted that we take separate cars, instead of me picking her up. Which was perfectly fine with me; just in case she was crazy. I always had to be on guard for the crazy type.

I arrived earlier than scheduled. I always liked to scope out the scene. See what I'm working with just in case I have to make a quick exit. I sat at our reserved table. I spotted her as soon as she walked through the door. Goddamn, she looked good! The scrubs I met her in didn't do any justice to her toned physique. I mean she was fine when I met her, but damn! The way this purple dress was hugging her breasts and ass, I could just imagine what she'd look like with that dress on the floor.

"Hi, D. Glove. How's it been?"

I stood up to hug her and pulled out her seat.

"Oh, such the gentleman."

I chuckled, "I try."

Our waiter returned, and we ordered drinks. I was going to order her a bottle of wine; but she told me after the week she's had, she needs something stronger. She ordered Hennessey on the rocks. Not a drink I would expect from a petite woman like her. But hey, I can't knock her because I ordered one myself.

"Tell me something about yourself Nurse Alicia."

"Hmm. Let's see. I'm 28 years old, an only child, and I'm a nurse at Texas Children's in the Medical Center. No kids, and I have a condo in midtown. What about you, D. Glove?"

"Well, I'm 33. I'll be 34 next month. No kids, have an older brother, and you already know I'm on the radio."

"Yes, and I make sure to never miss a show. I can't believe I'm listening to this voice face to face; instead of over my radio."

"Well, I hope I don't disappoint."

"So far, you haven't disappointed at all. Your chocolate skin, perfect white teeth, and muscles are perfect! You're tall, dark, and handsome. Just like I like 'em."

I smiled at her description of me.

Our food finally arrived. And as always, when food arrives, all conversation stops. But tonight, that wasn't the case. Alicia continued talking.

"Tell me how it is working and meeting all those stars."

Her eyes lit up when she said "stars". In between chews, I tried responding to her.

"Well, it's a very fun and interesting job. I do get a chance to meet a lot of the celebrities; and have even become close friends with some of them. But to me, they are just regular people like you and me."

Alicia continued talking about how excited she would be if she had a chance to meet all these celebrities. She barely ate anything because she talked so damn much. I was ready to end this date, and hopefully get back to her place. She finally took a break from talking and focused on her food. But that did not last for too long.

"So, is there a woman I need to be concerned with?" She asked.

"Nope, not one at all. I have friends, but that's it. Nothing serious. What about yourself?"

She rolled her eyes.

"Nope, no man over here. Men are just full of shit these days. All they want is your money, car, or pussy. I just got out of my relationship about two months ago. My boyfri—I mean my *ex-boyfriend* of 5 years was only with me for my money. Don't ask me why I stayed with him. He did not have a job, car, or anything of value to bring to the table. Sat in my condo all day, doing nothing; and I funded his ass. While I struggled through nursing school, he did nothing. While I busted my ass finding a job, he did nothing. While I bust my ass pulling overnight shifts at the hospital, he does nothing. Then he had the nerve to cheat on me. When I found out he had a 6-month-old baby, I couldn't take it anymore! Can you believe his baby mama showed up on my doorstep demanding money! So, yea, I kicked his ass out. And am finally doing me. Men are all fucking dogs!!"

Alicia had to stop and take a breather; she was so angry. The fact that she let a man lay up in her home while she brought home the bacon was absurd to me; but I kept that comment to myself. I apologized for his foolishness and tried to shift the conversation. I asked her what she liked to do for fun to lighten the mood. She told me she liked a few things, which one of the things reminded her of her ex. And just like that, she was back to talking about him again.

My phone started buzzing. I looked at it, and it was my brother. I saw this as my opportunity to exit stage left.

I answered the phone and put it on speakerphone.

"Hey D, you good?"

My brother and I had a system where if I ever picked up the phone and asked if he was good; he knew to respond with a sad or fake story.

"Nah man. 'Lisa ass locked me out of the house; knowing I forgot my key at home. I have to grab these documents and need to get back to the office in an hour. Can you please come unlock my door for me? I need you bro, please?"

I responded with, "Man, I'm on a date; I'm tied up right now."

Him knowing what to do; he kept egging it on.

"I'm really sorry to interrupt your date; but if I don't get these papers back to the office tomorrow morning; my head will be on a platter!"

I looked up at Alicia and shook my head in fake disbelief.

"Okay man; I'll hit you back. I'm about to wrap it up."

I hung up the phone and told Alicia that I was truly sorry; but I needed to help my brother. I flagged down our waiter, gave him two hundred dollars; and told him to keep the change. I apologized to Alicia; and told her that I must attend to my brother. She initially gave me grief about it; but said she understood. I told her that I didn't want to ruin her night and would hope that she could still enjoy herself. Alicia said she would move to the bar and cap off her night there. I kissed her on the forehead and walked away. I stopped at the bathroom, and when I came back out; Alicia had already began complaining about her ex-boyfriend to the bartender. I laughed, shook my head; and bolted out the door. I called my brother back to see what he really wanted. All he wanted to know was if I caught the Rocket's game.

I debated on going to Carmen's home. I sure thought I was going to get me some tonight. I was in the mood for sex but shook it off. I decided against it and went to The Roof in Sugarland. Figured I could just chill the night away and catch some live music.

As I was walking in, two beautiful women were walking out. But one of them really caught my eye. She was a pretty, mocha brown woman. Her skin was kissed by the sun, and her smile was beautiful. Her hair natural, full and pulled back into a high ponytail. was pulled back in a slick ponytail. And she was dressed in a navy-blue Polo shirt, jeans, and white Converse tennis. Body was thick and curvy in all the right places! Her and her friend were laughing as they walked out of the door. I don't think they even noticed me. I wanted to go after her but decided against it. I wasn't in the mood for another disappointment. I already took my L for the night.

I went to the bar and ordered me a Crown on the rocks. Once I got my drink, I went out on the roof top and jammed to some music. I zoned out and enjoyed the rest of my night, sipping and vibing.

Chapter 5

Tiffany

August 2017

It had been over six months, and things were still shaky with my sister. Many of days I tried calling her; but she wouldn't answer. I even took a trip back to Montgomery two months ago to talk to her face to face; but she avoided me. My mama set up a Sunday dinner for us to hash out our issues; but Tracy never showed. We went over to her house to pop up on her; but she wasn't home. I stayed for two weeks; hoping she would give in and meet with me. But it never happened. My mama tried her hardest to make things right, but Tracy wasn't budging. I didn't want to give up on her or our relationship, but what was I supposed to do?

Things with Calvin were also a little shaky. That was another reason I took a trip back to Montgomery. I needed family love and support. Numerous times, Calvin would disappear for hours. He would always say he was doing something for work. Also, whenever there was a work event; I was never invited. He said that since he was new; he was not allowed to have a "plus one". It just did not sit right with me. And it seems like things got worse since I have arrived back from Montgomery. We stopped having sex with one another completely. At first it would be a couple weeks here and there. But now it was months. Every time I would try, he always gave some excuse as to why he was not able to. Either he was too tired from work; was working on research, etc.

I felt so alone and isolated. Both my sister and husband were both putting me off.

Fortunately, my relationship had grew with Lauren. I was happy to have met her. With the distance between my sister and I; it was nice to have a girl-friend I could depend on. And with my husband spending so much time away from home; it was nice to have someone I could go out and occupy my time with.

Tonight, I was home alone like many other nights. I walked into the living room and turned on the television. I turned the channel to the local news because they were tracking and covering Hurricane Harvey all week. The hurricane was scheduled to hit Houston tonight. Luckily, I went to the store earlier last week to prepare myself. The hurricane was brining heavy rain and it was expected to cause flooding. Calvin along with the rest of the news crew were staying in a hotel together just in case flooding hit the city and people were not able to move around from their neighborhoods. I asked if spouses were able to come along also, but of course, he said he wasn't allowed to bring me. But this time, the excuse was because they were pairing anchors up per room to save on hotel room costs. So yet again, I was left alone. And I was going to have to ride this hurricane out by myself. Tonight, was going to be a Cabernet and takeout kind of night.

After eating dinner, I showered and stretched out on the sofa. I popped a bag of popcorn and poured another glass of Cabernet. Like any other Friday night at 8PM, I turned on Netflix for my weekly movie night. I felt the wine working on me and drifted off to sleep before the credits finished rolling.

I was later awakened by what sounded like a train passing in front of the house. I looked at the clock, and it was 1:23AM. I ran to the window, and saw debris flying around the neighborhood. I rubbed my eyes and realized the debris was from my neighbors' roof that was ripped from their homes. And that train sound I was hearing was the wind. It was also beginning to flood in the neighborhood, but it hadn't reached the area in front of my home.

I instantly panicked and called Calvin. No answer. I called again. No answer. I started to cry because I was afraid of what this hurricane could do to our home. What it could do to me.

And I had no one here to protect me. I went back in the living room and turned the television back to the news. I saw Calvin sitting at the anchors desk covering the story. That explained why he did not answer my call. I felt some comfort being able to see his face on the TV screen.

"We are being told that Hurricane Harvey has made landfall and is destroying homes across the city. PXBN Channel 3's Tabitha Dixon, is live in the Meyerland area. With the very latest on tracking this destructive hurricane, here's Tabitha."

The camera flipped to live coverage, and what I saw nearly stopped my heart. And it was *not* the hurricane! It was her. The woman I saw on Tracy's cell phone, rubbing and kissing all over Calvin. I never knew her name, but today I read it clear as day. Tabitha Dixon! I walked closer to the television to make sure. *It was her!* What the hell?! I couldn't believe that she was here! I thought I would be getting away from her. Has she been here all this time? Have I never noticed her before? Was Calvin still sleeping with her? So many questions started running through my mind, and I needed answers. I blew up Calvin's phone. Called him well over 50 times, and I received no answer. I got lightheaded and sat down at the kitchen table. I felt like I was out of breath. I tried opening a bottle of water but did not have the strength to open it. My body felt restless.

I felt like I was going to die. I could not breathe. I looked back at the television and her face seemed as if it was taunting me. I grabbed my phone and called Lauren. She didn't answer. I looked at the time again, and realized she was probably asleep. I mustered up the strength to stand and grabbed my keys. I figured I would just show up at her place. I needed someone to talk to. Desperately! I opened the door and was soon reminded that we were in the middle of a hurricane. More debris was floating around in the air, trees were swaying back and forth, and water was coming down the street. There was no way I could drive in this condition. I then saw someone else's roof beginning to rip from their home. I let out a scream and slammed the door. I fell to the floor and curled into a ball. I then began to sob.

I felt so alone. I felt heartbroken. My breathing became jaded again. The more I tried to catch my breath, the harder it became to breathe. I started wheezing and hyperventilating until I passed out.

I woke up the next morning in the same position as the night before. It was still raining outside, but at least I wasn't hearing those strong winds anymore. I looked at my phone. Calvin didn't call me back. I called him again, and he still didn't answer. I saw Lauren called me 5 times, so I called her back.

"Hey girl, sorry I missed your call. That rain knocked me out. How are you holding up over there? I heard Sienna

Plantation got hit pretty hard last night, and I have been worried about you ever since. Did you suffer any damage? We have flooding over in my subdivision, but no wind damage."

I opened my mouth to speak, but no words came out.

"Hello? Tiffany, you there?"

"Lauren." My voice was shaky.

"Tiffany girl, what's wrong? Are you okay? Are you safe?"

"She's here."

"Who's here?"

"Tabitha."

"Who's Tabitha?"

"She's the woman Calvin cheated on me with, I found out her name last night."

"How do you know that? Are you sure?"

"I saw her on the news last night. She was covering the hurricane. She works with Calvin. They work at the same damn station! I'm sure they are still seeing each other. What is she doing here, Lauren? She is not supposed to be here! I thought we left her in Montgomery!"

I began to sob again and started hyperventilating again.

"Breathe, Tiffany. Catch your breath honey."

I managed to calm myself down.

"Have you tried reaching out to Calvin?"

"I called him all night and he never answered. I even called this morning and he still didn't answer."

"I'm so, so sorry my friend. I wish I could be there to give you a hug, but my neighborhood is flooded."

"I understand."

"Let's facetime. We can pour us a drink, and you tell me all about it. I'm here for you friend."

I saw the notification that Lauren was trying to Face Time. I answered and managed to get myself off the floor.

"You going to pour up?" Lauren asked.

"It's too early. I'm just going to lay on the couch here."

"Ok, do whatever is comfortable for you."

I laid down on the couch and began rubbing my temples.

"Now tell me what happened, Tiff."

2 Weeks Later

It has been two weeks since Hurricane Harvey made landfall, and I still haven't heard from Calvin. I called him numerous times, and it was going straight to voicemail. Yet, I saw him every night on the news. So, I knew he had to be avoiding me. I started seeing Tabitha reporting the weather more as well. I kept questioning how and why I have not seen her any other time until Hurricane Harvey. Where has she been all this time? I wasn't sure what to make out of this situation. I wasn't sure what was going on with my marriage. I didn't know what to think. I did have a feeling something bad was soon going to happen though.

On the bright side, the flooding went down, and the sun

finally came out yesterday. The city was getting back to normal. I could not wait to get out of this house and focus my energy onto something else. I asked Lauren if we could go out for brunch and drinks. Of course, she agreed. If liquor and food were involved; she was in there. I headed to pick her up.

We soon arrived at Phil and Derek's. The place was packed! I'm sure everyone was happy to get out of the house and enjoy this sunshine on a Saturday afternoon. The hostess sat us at the bar, and we ordered Mimosa's to start. Our waiter returned with our drinks.

"How are you holding up, friend? Still no sight or a response from Calvin?"

"Nope. I don't know what the hell to think anymore. I'm scared that something isn't right. I just can't put my finger on it. And then, I get angry because--. You know what? I don't want to go down that road. How have you been? How's your neighborhood been since the flooding went down?"

After catching up with small talk, we headed to the other side of the restaurant where people were partying and dancing. Texas music was so different than what I'm used to back in Alabama. As we were dancing and having a good time; I looked over and saw a man staring at me. I brushed it off and quickly looked away. I didn't want to keep looking and have him thinking he could ask me for my number. I tucked my hair behind my ear; hoping he would notice my wedding ring.

After enough talking, eating, drinking, and dancing; we were ready to go. I flagged down our waiter to pay our ticket.

"Oh no friend. I'll get it this time. You've been through it these past two weeks, let me treat you."

"No, I dragged you out of the house to meet me and discuss all my drama and shit. I got it."

I gave the waiter my card. He then left, but soon returned.

"Your card has been declined, ma'am. Do you have another one you want to try?"

"I don't have another card. Can you try it again, maybe it was an error?"

"I tried three times ma'am. And each time it declined."

"Here you go, try this one." Lauren pulled out her card and gave it to the waiter.

I checked my account on the mobile app, and the balance was $0.00. What the fuck? Why was my account empty? Did somebody hack into my account?

"I'm going to go to the bathroom and call my bank. Be right back."

I ran off to the bathroom and called the bank.

"Hi, this is Tiffany Willow. My account balance is showing that I don't have any money in my account. Can you tell me what is going on?"

"Mrs. Willow, your husband emptied out this account yesterday evening right before closing. Said y'all were going with a new bank. You weren't aware?"

"No, I was not aware. Did he say which bank?"

"No ma'am, he did not."

"Thank you."

I instantly hung up the phone and shouted, "FUCK!" I dazed out for a second and received an alert from my phone. It was a notification from our security system. *Motion detected at Garage.* Then another notification came in. *Motion detected at Front Door.* Then another one. *Front Door Open.* I clicked on the notification and it showed Calvin walking through the front door. I then clicked on the Garage camera, and I could see Tabitha sitting in Calvin's car in our driveway. She then got out of the car and was walking to the front door. Was he really bringing this bitch to our home? I ran out of the bathroom and down the hallway. I then bumped into someone. I tripped over him and almost took him down with me. He helped me up back on my feet.

"I'm so sorry!"

"It's okay. You good?"

"Yea, I'm fine."

I quickly walked off back to where Lauren was. She was signing the receipt.

"Did you find out what happened?"

"This motherfucker cleaned out my bank account. And he's at the house right now with that bitch! We have to leave.

Now!"

"Aww shit. Here we go."

I was driving like a bat out of hell, flying down Hwy 59 South. What would normally take thirty-five minutes, took twenty. I arrived at our home and irately pulled up on the lawn. I jumped out of the car and began running towards the door. Lauren got out of the car and followed behind me. I stopped when I saw Tabitha sitting in the passenger seat. I grabbed on her door, but she locked it.

"Get out of the car, bitch!"

I started banging on the car window and noticed Calvin walking out of the house with a suitcase. I started charging towards him. He stopped in his tracks when he saw me approaching him.

"What the fuck is going on here, Calvin?"

"Tiffany, what does it look like is going on?"

"You're leaving? Where the hell are you going?"

"I can't do this anymore, Tiffany. Things are not working between us anymore, and I just can't fake it any longer. We tried; we really did. All the therapy, all the seminars, all the retreats. It only puts a temporary band-aid on it. But you and I know it's not worth it."

"So, it's like that? You just pack up and leave? You give up?"

"What's left for me to give? Look, I am going to Tabitha's

for the week. I am giving you seven days. When I return, I want you out of here. And if you think of having an Angela Basset's "Waiting to Exhale" moment and do any damage to this house; the station will sue you."

Tears welled up in my eyes. I knew things were bad, but not this bad. Calvin continued on.

"I cannot keep subjecting myself to this. To you. I want more for myself and for the woman I am with. It's over Tiffany."

"Let's talk about this, Calvin. We can try therapy again. We can work through this together. Please don't give up on us Calvin."

"Come on Tiffany. You had to know I was not happy. We have not slept together in months, and I have been gone since the Hurricane. What did you think was going on?"

"I uprooted my life and came to Houston for you. I quit my job for you. You told me I did not have to work. And then you clear out my account and leave me with nothing? You know I do not have any money to get a place. What am I supposed to do? Where am I supposed to go?"

"I don't know, Tiffany. I'm giving you seven days to stay here and figure it out. Call your family and have them get you a ticket to go back home. You don't have a reason to be here now."

Rage came over me, and I pounced on Calvin like a lion

would on his prey. Those Kickboxing classes came in handy. We fell to the ground, and I continued wailing on him in between him blocking my blows. Lauren ran up and pulled me off of Calvin. Tabitha got out of the car and went to Calvin to console him. I then snatched her by her hair and started wailing on her too. It took Lauren and Calvin to pull me off of her.

"Let me go! Let me go!" I screamed as they held me back. "This the bitch you want, huh? This raggedy head bitch?" I held up the weave I snatched from Tabitha's head.

"See, I wasn't going to take it there. But there you go putting your hands on people! You want to know why I'm leaving you, Tiffany? You are not the same girl I met when we were in high school. You let yourself go. You got boring. We went off to college with big dreams. We both started off together in the same field. Yet, I soared, and you stayed the same. You stayed behind the scenes and you never wanted more for yourself. And it carried over into every other aspect of your life. You only dress up if I initiate it. You rarely get your hair done. You let weeks go by before you get a fresh manicure and pedicure. You are always wearing jeans and t shirts. It's like I'm with one of the boys."

I started to cry. Hearing those words cut deep. Yet, Calvin continued on.

"And you call her raggedy? At least she knows how to keep a man. She fixes herself up. She takes the time to do the little things to wow me. She has a big career. She is going places. She makes me feel alive and excites me. Unlike you."

I stared at Calvin in disbelief. I could not believe he was saying all of these things to me. Like I was some bitch off the street. Like I have not given him 13 years of my life. I looked over at Tabitha, and she was standing there with a smug look on her face. Like she was proud of taking my husband from me.

My breathing became jaded. I felt like another panic attack was coming over me. I stood there, crying, breathing distorted; feeling like I was about to die. Again.

"Look at you, speechless. That'll teach you to put your hands on me again."

Just when I felt like I was going to faint, Lauren walked up behind me and held me by the shoulders.

"Pack your things, Tiffany! You do not have to deal with this shit. You are better than this. You're coming with me!"

"Listen to your friend, Tiffany."

"Shut the fuck up, you low life piece of shit!" Lauren said in my honor.

Calvin smirked then told Tabitha to get in the car. He picked up the suitcase and put it in the car. They got in and drove off. I watched them drive down the street and then turn out the subdivision. I looked around the neighborhood, and at least ten different neighbors were outside, witnessing everything that took place.

"What the fuck are y'all staring at?" I screamed to the neighbors. Most of them scurried back into their homes, while the others stood firm, staring at me in disbelief.

"Let's get in the house, friend."

Lauren helped me walk into the house. I dropped down to my knees and started crying.

"What is going on, Lauren? How is this my life? How did this happen? What did I do to deserve this?"

I continued crying. I looked up and Lauren was crying with me.

"I'm so sorry Tiffany. I cannot believe this is happening to you. There are no other words to say but bad things happen to good people. And you, are indeed a good person. This is not your fault. You did nothing wrong. Let's pack up your belongings and get out of here."

Lauren helped me pack up some of my clothes and other belongings. I fit what I could in the suitcases I had, but this was nowhere near all of my things. I let her drive my car back to her home. I dazed out and looked out of the window the whole ride to her house. I kept replaying in my mind what just took place.

We arrived at her house shortly after, and brought my belongings in.

"What you want to do friend? Talk, shower, eat, go to

sleep? You tell me what you're in the mood for."

"I just want to shower and go to sleep."

"Okay, I have extra towels and soap in the linen closet. Make yourself at home."

I dug into my suitcase and pulled out some clothes for after my shower. I got a towel and a bar of soap and headed into the bathroom. I placed my things on the counter and turned on the shower. I looked in the mirror and wanted to scream. I felt horrible. I felt low. I felt like trash. I felt alone. I took off my clothes and got in the shower. The tears never stopped flowing. I couldn't tell if it was my tears or the shower water puddling up around my feet. I covered my mouth and wailed to myself. I couldn't believe my marriage ended the way it just did.

Chapter 6

Tiffany

September 2017

I woke up and realized I was sleeping on Lauren's couch. I moved three states away just to be sleeping on a friend's couch. I was so grateful to Lauren; but was upset that this was my life. I looked around and saw my clothes overstuffed in suitcases. I could not believe that this has happened to me another time! Calvin strikes again! How could the man I love and put all of my devotion into continue to treat me as a rag doll?! How could I be so stupid to allow this man to keep cheating on me?

It had been a week since the blow up with Calvin. Even though I felt like a fool, I needed answers and called Calvin continuously. Just to get sent to voicemail. At one point it, it started going straight to voicemail without it even ringing. I texted him as well. Only to receive messages back asking me to stop calling and texting him. He also told me that he would be filing for divorce soon.

I know that I lost my way over the years, I can admit that. Working in a male dominated industry like sports can do that to a woman. I started off going to work looking cute and made up. But I started dressing plain after being hit on all the time. I guess I did not notice that it carried over into my life outside of work. I just wished that he would have articulated that to me. I could have changed. I could have been better. I could have given him what he wanted and needed from me. If I would have known, it would lead to him leaving me; I would have fixed it with the quickness.

Then I started to think that Tracy was right all along. She always reminded me how I helped him get in the position that he was in. How I coached him on speaking and engaging with his audience. How to walk in a room and command it. And he used that against me in the long run. Tracy made me feel good about myself; pumped up my self-esteem. And I pushed her away. She also told me what kind of man I had. And instead of believing her; I again pushed her away and stood by him. I let him create a wedge between my sister and me. How could I be so naïve? She gave me proof; hardcore proof with Tabitha that I saw with my own eyes. And I still took him back. I felt so dumb, so used, so violated. I wanted to call her, but I felt so ashamed. I could not admit to her that Calvin cheated again with the same woman. I couldn't face her.

To make things even worse, yesterday was my birthday. I spent my birthday heartbroken and crying my eyes out instead of a romantic dinner at a nice restaurant, across the table from my husband. Reality set in and tears welled up in my eyes. I sat there and cried like a baby. Lauren came over to me and patted me on the shoulder.

"Tiffany honey, it will be alright."

I quickly wiped my tears.

"Sorry Lauren, I didn't mean to wake you with my sobbing."

Lauren shook her head and smiled.

"No honey, it's okay. I was in your shoes once before. I know exactly what you are going through. And you have nothing to apologize for. Cry all you need to. And if you need someone to talk to, I'm here."

I thanked Lauren for her kind words. Lauren told me that she was about to make breakfast and asked if I would like some. As sad as I was, I was just as hungry. I got up and followed Lauren into the kitchen.

I looked around Lauren's condo. She had it nicely decorated. It made me sad because Lauren had started helping me decorate my place. Well, it was not *my* place anymore. It was Calvin's place. The house was coming together, and we only had a few more pieces to buy until it was complete. I cannot believe that bastard told me if I damaged anything, I would be sued. I worked so damn hard to make that house pretty. Just for it to be shared and enjoyed with another woman.

I sat on the bar stool and watched Lauren prepare breakfast. Emotions started to build up inside of me again.

"How could I be so stupid Lauren? Not once, but twice this man has been caught with this woman. I cannot believe he played me like this. Dragged me all the way to Houston, just to toss me out like a piece of trash. I could have stayed in Montgomery for all of this. I have been debating back and forth; but I am going to call my mother later today. I will ask her to send me some money for a plane ticket back to Montgomery. Might as well take my butt back home and beg my old supervisor for my job back."

While scrambling eggs, Lauren turned to me.

"You're not a fool honey. You are supposed to trust your husband. Nothing wrong with trusting the man you committed your life to before God and your family." Lauren fixed my plate and put it down in front of me. "And if it makes you feel any better, I'm happy to have met you. You have been a wonderful friend to me. You are a great woman, and you deserve better. Hell, who knows. You may find you a good man here. Houston does have over 5 million residents. I'm sure you'll meet somebody who will make you feel like the Black Queen you are. Now dry them tears and don't let another one fall for Calvin. Stop doubting yourself and stop letting him get the best of you. You are more than what he said about you. You are Tiffany Goddam Willow! Shape up, friend!"

Lauren brought me a glass of orange juice.

"Now eat this food before it gets cold. Then, get dressed. I promised you I would get you a job, and I will hold up to my promise."

Lauren and I had breakfast and then parted to get ready for the day. Lauren did promise to get me a job at one of the local radio stations as a radio engineer. She said the manager was a client of hers, and she put in a good word for me. She was most certain that the job was mine. To be honest, I didn't think I would get the job. I had such a big gap in my employment history. I hadn't worked in months. I was rusty. I am sure there was someone else who was more qualified than I was, and I was also sure this manager was not going to consider me. I was only going because I did not want to disappoint Lauren. But I had already made up my mind. I was calling my mother and would have to face her and the rest of my family when I got back home.

I went back to the couch and started digging through my suitcase. After a long while of digging, I managed to pull out a decent interview outfit. I ironed, got dressed, then went into her bedroom and did a spin in front of Lauren.

"So, what do you think?"

"I think you're going to get the job! You look good, girl. Let's roll."

She grabbed her keys and we headed out to the car.

Lauren and I arrived at the radio station, called The Groove. I am a SIRIUS Radio kind of girl, so I rarely listen to the radio. Too many damn ads and commercials.

We walked into the building and rode the elevator up to fifth floor. Lauren could see the nerves written over my face. She held my hand and told me I got this. I smiled at her, and we stepped off the elevator. It was a nice, fancy office. Way different than what I was used to at ASU. Everyone seemed to be friendly. We walked through the lobby and sat in the waiting area outside of the manager's office. He soon stepped out.

"Hello there, Lauren. How are you? My wife told me to tell you she would be calling you soon. She's now remodeling the guest suite and needs your help."

"How are you, Jeff? Tell her I will be looking forward to her call." She then focused on me. "Here is the radio engineer I was telling you about."

I smiled and introduced myself. We then shook hands.

"Hi, Mrs. Willow. Nice to meet you. Can you go into my office and make yourself comfortable? I will be there in a sec."

I walked into his office and took a seat. I heard Lauren outside talking to him, and the conversation seemed very pleasant. He then came in and closed the door behind him.

"Sorry I was so focused on Lauren out there and didn't properly greet you. But my wife has been on my tail about making sure I talked to Lauren about that guest suite. I had to tell her before I forgot."

"It's okay." I chuckled.

He then extended his hand for me to shake. I extended mines and we shook hands.

"Nice to meet you again, Mrs. Willow. I'm Jeffrey Patterson."

"Hi, Mr. Patterson. Again, I'm Tiffany Willow."

"Call me Jeff." He said with a smile.

He sat down and looked over my resume. He then asked me a few standard questions. I explained to him that I graduated with my Bachelor's in Communications from Alabama State University and have been working in the sports department since my junior year. I explained that I recently left the station last year; due to moving to Houston for a bigger market.

Mr. Patterson pointed to the degree behind him.

"What does that degree say, baby girl?" I looked up at the degree. A smile came across my face.

"You went to Alabama State also?"

"You damn right! No other school is better! Is Mr. Abrams still the overhead there?"

"Stop it. You worked with Mr. Abrams too?!" I said with excitement.

"Yep, he taught me everything I know about the radio industry."

"Wow! I love Mr. Abrams. He was so sad to see me go. He was like a second father to me."

"Yes, that man has raised us all. Well, it's nothing left to say, but welcome to the station. My fellow Hornet!"

Mr. Patterson stood up and extended his hand for me to shake it and seal the deal.

"Thank you so much! I can't wait to join the team!"

Mr. Patterson went into more detail of the job position and description. He explained that I would work the late shift. Which was from 7PM to 12AM. At this point, I did not care what the hours were. I am willing to work any schedule to get back on my feet. The job was set to start in two weeks so I guess I wouldn't be calling my mother for that plane ticket after all.

Lauren and I went out to celebrate my birthday and new job offer. It felt good knowing I was going to be a working woman again. Making my own money, calling my own shots. I messed up and let Calvin convince me to quit my job. Convince me that he would take care of me. What a big mistake! He was able to control my money; and took it all from me when he chose to. Never again.

Over dinner and drinks, Lauren and I came up with a 6-month plan now that I had a job and planned on staying in Houston. She had a second room that was a home office. She was going to rearrange it and convert it into a bedroom for me. She agreed to let me stay rent and utility free. I offered to pay, but she insisted that I didn't have to. She just wanted me to get on my feet and was happy that she could be of assistance.

I swallowed my pride and reached out to Calvin again. I damn near begged him to let me come over and get the rest of my things. I only grabbed a few things that day I left. I scrambled as much as I could and flew out of there. But now I needed the rest of my clothes and other belongings since I was starting this new life without him. I left him a long voicemail and text message. A few days later he responded and told me I could come over Thursday while he was at work and gather the rest of my things. The bastard then told me to leave my key on the kitchen table on my way out. He also reminded me if I did anything to damage the home, the station would sue me. What an asshole! As much as I wanted to curse him out, I dismissed that thought. I just wanted my belongings.

When Thursday came, Lauren and I went over to my old home. She let me use a couple of her vans from her designing company. Along with a couple of her company movers.

I opened the front door and was instantly greeted with sadness and hurt. It was weird that I once called this place home, and now I felt like a guest here. I walked through the living room, and saw glasses left out on the counter. One of the glasses had lipstick around it. I picked it up and looked at it. The lipstick looked fresh. Like last night, fresh. This bastard had this bitch all up in my space. Drinking wine from glasses I purchased. I shook it off and continued throughout the house.

Over the next few hours, I packed up all of my clothes, shoes, purses, jewelry, and other accessories. Most of my belongings had been placed in the guest room, while Tabitha's clothes were in the main bedroom. I also took a good amount of the things I bought when Lauren and I went out shopping for home décor. We loaded it all onto the vans. Good thing she let me borrow them.

Well, that was everything. I took one last look around the house before leaving out. I took the house keys off my key ring and set it down on the table. I left and accepted whatever life had to throw at me next.

Chapter 7

D. Glove

October 2017

Today was the day that our permanent engineer was supposed to start. The position was officially filled. I was happy that we were finally done with the intern. I was hoping that the new engineer had the same work ethic, or at least close to Mr. Thomas. I walked into the studio, and the engineer booth was still empty. Within the next five minutes, a woman dressed in jeans and a t-shirt walked into the suite. She was carrying a huge box covering her face. I was surprised that a package was being delivered this late.

I went to the door to help her with the box.

"Let me get that for you, ma'am."

"Thank you. Wish you could've met me downstairs. That thing is heavy." She joked as she handed me the box.

Damn! This was the same woman I seen walking out of

The Roof that one night I went. And she was the woman who almost knocked me down in the hallway at Phil and Derek's. She was still the most beautiful woman that I have ever seen! I was face to face with that decadent, mocha skin, and beautiful smile again.

"Hi, I'm Tiffany. Your new engineer." She said as she reached out her hand for me to shake it.

And here I am thinking she's from FedEx or something.

I motioned that I could not shake her hand because I was holding the box, and we chuckled together. For a quick second, I was shocked that this would be the new person that I would have to work with. I questioned if I would be able to maintain myself working with her.

"Hi, Tiffany. My name is Darryl Glover, and I host the Midnight Love segment."

We exchanged pleasantries of how happy we were to start working together. I waited to see if she would recognize me from that incident; but she never brought it up. As flustered as she was that day; I am sure she probably forgot.

"Let me show you to your booth."

Tiffany trailed behind me as I walked her into the engineer's booth. I placed her box on her new desk.

"I tried fixing up the room before you got here; I hope you like it."

Tiffany did a spin around the room and looked around.

"Yes, I like what you have done with it. Thanks for hooking it up for me."

I asked Tiffany if she wanted me to give her a tour around the building. Tiffany laughed and said that she needed to know where the bathroom was before anything. I instructed Tiffany to the restroom and told her that I would be here waiting for her to get back. A quick five minutes passed, and Tiffany walked back into the studio. I then took Tiffany throughout the building, showing her around.

"So, what made you come to the radio station?"

Tiffany hesitated, but then finally answered.

"I have been in sports communication for a while, and finally wanted to switch over to the music industry. I just want to be well rounded within my career."

She then went on to explain that she was from Alabama but moved here at the top of the year. Said she wanted a change of scenery and more career opportunities. I explained to her that I was born and raised in Houston and couldn't imagine living anywhere but the H. So, I was proud of her for making such a big change. I welcomed her to the city.

We made it back to the studio from our quick tour. I told her that I liked for my 'Midnight Love' mood to be set with candles and a dimly lit room. I asked her if that would be a problem.

"I'm in your world and will follow suit. Whatever pleases

you is fine with me."

Hearing those words gave me goosebumps. I liked Tiffany's vibe. She seemed very mature, and cool to be around. Tiffany walked over to the production center and started messing with the different knobs and buttons. I could see she knew what she was doing. Way better than the last engineer we had. She asked if we could do a test run before the shift started. I said sure and went to my seat. Tiffany troubleshooted a few things until she finally had it adjusted to her likening. I asked if everything was all good, and she thumbs-up. I then began my daily routine of starting up my segment.

"Alright, alright. It's Midnight Love, with ya boy D. Glove. Turning up this Houston heat, while you lay in your sheets. Giving you the smoothest tunes, hoping to put you in the groove."

I looked over at Tiffany, and she had her headphones in; focused.

"I first want to open the show, letting you guys know that after almost a year of our beloved Mr. Thomas being happy and retired from the station, we finally have our new permanent engineer. Everybody welcome Tiffany to the FXLV family!"

I clapped and glanced back at Tiffany. She sat in the booth with her headphones on and gave a thumbs up to me. I then went on and did my segment bit.

The show was over at midnight. I cleared out my space, and Tiffany came out of the booth. After packing up our things, we started walking towards the parking garage.

"So, how was your first day? I hope those callers weren't too much for you. They can get a little crazy and raunchy these hours of the night."

Tiffany chuckled to herself.

"Yes, those women were bold! They are basically throwing themselves at you over the phone."

"Yea, I've learned over the years that a lot of these women are lonely and look forward to hearing me every night. Some have even told me they love when I come on air because I'm the only constant man in their life. They know they can catch me every night from 7pm-12am."

"Damn, that's crazy. I thought that was just for the movies, but women really fall for the radio guy huh?"

"Damn, I'm just a radio guy?"

I joked with her. She blushed.

"Sorry, I didn't mean it like that."

"I know what you meant; I'm just kidding. But to answer your question, yes some women really play into this fantasy of lusting over the radio guy they hear every night."

Tiffany shook her head and chuckled to herself.

"So, are you driving or is someone coming to pick you up?" I asked.

"I'm driving myself."

"Where's your car?"

"Top floor. The lot was packed earlier. So, I guess the evening shift was still here, because all of the cars are gone now."

"Yea I'm sure if you wait about 10 minutes before coming in, some cars will clear out and you can get you a better spot. But not this one."

I pointed to my car.

"*This* spot is courtesy of being the top radio personality at the station." I joked.

"So, you're flexing right now since you got curbside service?" She said as she laughed.

"Just a little." I laughed back with her.

I let her know that I could drive her to her car; but that the company also had a security officer named Mr. Freddy, that could escort her as well. Tiffany said that she would go with the security officer. Tiffany thanked me for showing her around on her first day, and that she would see me tomorrow. I said the same, and we both walked away.

"Hey Darryl, on another note; I'll take you up on that ride."

Tiffany walked back over to my car. I opened her door, and she hopped right in. We drove up to the top floor, and she pointed out her car.

"The gray Malibu to your right."

We pulled up to her car, and I could tell she wasn't eager to get out. Like she wasn't ready to go home. I figured I'd try my luck.

"Hey, since you're fairly new to town, let me take you out for a bite to eat at one of our top black spots. Have you ever been to The Breakfast Klub?"

"Nope, but I've heard so much about it. And I've always wanted to go."

"Well, let me treat you to a good meal."

"You don't have to get home? It won't be too much of a bother?"

"Nah, nothing at home waiting for me but a bowl of cereal and Martin on BET."

She laughed.

"Okay, cool. I'll follow you out."

Tiffany got out of my car and hopped into hers. When I saw she was ready, I drove off and she followed behind me.

We arrived at The Breakfast Klub, and like all other times, we had to wait in line. Tiffany took this time to check out the menu.

"Ooh, this Katfish and Grits looks delicious. Have you ever tried it? Will you recommend it?"

"I'm a Wings & Waffle kind of man, but the Katfish and Grits are good too."

We made it to the front of the line and placed our orders. We then got our drinks and found a seat.

"I was waiting to see if you would say anything, but you don't remember me. Do you?"

Tiffany looked at me for a while, then shook her head no.

"Phil and Derek's? When you came out of the bathroom, cursing and then you tripped? Flew into my arms and almost knocked us both down? We also locked eyes while you were out on the dance floor."

I could see it all coming back to Tiffany from the expression on her face. She then burst into laughter.

"Oh my God! That was you?! I was so into my own shit; I didn't even look at you! I'm so embarrassed." Tiffany continued laughing.

"There's nothing to be embarrassed about. Now, if we actually fell; then you would have something to be embarrassed about." I joked.

Tiffany was still laughing to herself. She was in tears by this time.

"My friend and I still laugh about that til this day. I can't believe that was you."

She finally stopped laughing and wiped her eyes.

"Yea, you almost took us out! Nah, but seriously. I also saw you before at The Roof months before Phil and Derek's. You were with a friend of yours."

"Yea, my friend Lauren likes to go there to listen to music. Wow, that's so ironic. Small world."

"Right. As big as Houston is; you always run into the same people. Small world indeed."

While we waited on our food, a few women passed by flirting. Making sure they brushed up against me.

"Well damn. Luckily, I'm your coworker, and not your woman. These women are disrespectful." Tiffany laughed at the women and their actions.

"Yea, being on the radio has it's perks here and there. Sometimes it's cute, sometimes it's desperate. But hey, what's a man supposed to do?"

"Hey, if I had the pick of the litter at my fingertips; I'd be in the same boat. I can't blame ya!"

I laughed at her realness.

"So, speaking of pick of the litter, there's no man waiting at home for you?"

Instantly, I could see Tiffany's demeanor change.

"You ok there, partner?" I genuinely asked out of concern.

"Yes, I'm okay. And no, I don't have anyone waiting at home for me. I'm actually going through a divorce. Well, he hasn't officially sent any paperwork over or anything. But we've been separated since Hurricane Harvey."

"Aww, sorry to hear that".

I really wasn't. That makes it easier for me to get her. But I played the part.

"No, it's okay. I've said too much. I don't want you to have any pity for me. That's not the first impression I want my new coworker to have of me."

"Aww girl, stop it. If you want to talk about it, I'm here. My brother was faced with a divorce some years ago, and it shook him to the core. So, I could only imagine what you're going through. If you need a listening ear, I'm here. Plus, I need to know who I'm working with, right? We stuck with each other every night from now on. I wanna get to know you."

I nudged her and smiled. Tiffany smiled back out of relief.

"Alright, here goes. I'll make this long story short. My husband cheated, got caught, and I took him back. We went to counseling, and I thought we worked out our issues. We packed up to move to Houston to better his career; only to find out his mistress lives here. After he realized he wants her more than me; he kicked me out and moved her in. And now here I am. In a brand-new city and state, no family, and having to fend for myself."

A singe tear rolled down Tiffany's face.

"Crazy thing is I'm still in love with him and want him back. But I'm trying to align life now without him."

Damn that's messed up, I thought.

"Aww partner. I feel for you. How are you holding up with a place to stay and finances?"

Tiffany dabbed her eyes with a napkin.

"Thank God I walked into a Kickboxing class my second day in Houston. I met the instructor, who then became a close friend of mine. She is my only friend here. Lauren, the woman you saw me with at The Roof and Phil and Derek's. When everything went down, she let me stay with her. And I'll be staying with her until I get on my feet. She's also the one who helped me get the job here. She knows Mr. Patterson."

"Well, I'm glad you have some support. Don't hesitate to call me if you need to. I'm here. You have a friend in me also."

"Thanks Darryl. Let's talk about something else. I didn't come here to bore you with my troubles."

Our food then arrived.

"Well, I hope this food cheer you up. I know you'll enjoy it."

For the next two hours, Tiffany and I ate and had good conversation. We both talked about our family the most. I told her about my brother Daniel and his wife Jalisa. I also told her about my parents, and how we were all a tight knit family. Tiffany told me about her family back in Alabama. She adored her parent's relationship also. And she also had one sibling like me, but a sister. Tiffany expressed that she hasn't spoke to her sister since January because of the relationship her sister and husband had. Tiffany also expressed how much it hurts that her relationship with her sister has yet to be repaired.

I found out that she lives on the Southwest with her friend; but planned to get herself a condo in River Oaks when she's able to afford her own place. I let her know that I lived on the West side of town, in the Memorial area. We went on and on, talking about our goals and ultimate career dreams.

I learned a lot about Tiffany during these two hours. I have never had such an intimate connection like that with a woman who I was not sleeping with. But something was different about Tiffany. She was down to earth, real, and authentic. She was not afraid to speak her mind; but knew how to not overdo it. I appreciated that in her. It was refreshing.

I checked my watch; it was going on 3:30AM.

"You need to get home, pretty lady. I did not plan on keeping you out this late."

Tiffany looked at her phone.

"Ooh yeah, I need to carry my butt on home."

We got up, left out, and walked back to our cars. Before she made it to her car, which was parked ahead of mine, she turned around.

"Darryl, thank you for the meal. And thank you for listening to me. I needed to get those things off my chest."

I smiled.

"Sure anytime. I hope things work out in your favor. Be

safe getting home, and I'll see you back at work tomorrow."

"Sure thing."

I watched as Tiffany walked to her car and pulled off. As I walked back to my car, I wish I would have gotten her number so she could let me know that she made it in safely.

First thing I did when I got in my car is call my brother. He picked up the phone and sounded groggy.

"Darryl, do you know what time it is man?"

I looked at the time in my car, *3:45AM*. I was so eager; I didn't even consider the time.

"Sorry, bro. I can call you back in the morning."

"Nah, tell me now. It must be urgent if you are calling at this time of night. You know Jalisa crazy. You're trying to get me cut!"

I chuckled because I know Jalisa does not play.

"Bro, I met a woman tonight man. I don't know what it is about her, but damn! I'm lowkey feeling her. And I can't stop thinking about what I want to do to her."

Daniel laughed.

"Another one? Man, what club you met her at this time?"

"Nah man. I met her at work. Remember I told you our new engineer was starting tonight? Well, I thought it was going to be another man. But it was her. Her name is Tiffany. We went out for breakfast after work, and I got to know her better."

"Whoa man, do you think that's cool? Are you sure that you want to get involved with someone you work with? That can get ugly with your track record."

"Damn, what's that supposed to mean?"

"Darryl, who do you think you're talking to? I am your brother, remember? I see how you smash and dash these women. I would hate for that to come back and bite you in the ass at your workplace. And just think, not only would you have to see her at work; you'll have to see her at all the extra gigs the station puts on. That could get messy."

I thought about it for a minute, and Daniel did have a point. I didn't want to have a crazy woman on my hands that I had to be around for hours on end.

"You are right bro. That could get messy. And that is not the end of it. She's still married but going through a divorce."

I could hear Daniel's tone change.

"Aww man, hell nah. That woman probably still in love with her husband; and her husband is probably still in love with her. That's how things go in a marriage. When Jalisa and I lost the baby last time, and she wanted to throw in the towel; I wasn't ready for it to end. I played it off and gave her the space she needed; but she was still my wife and I treated her as such. I wish I did hear about her dating a new guy. I would've beat his ass for touching my woman. You do not need a crazy husband stalking you or trying to harm you."

"But that's two different situations. *He* was in the wrong here. *He* wants to throw in the towel."

"It doesn't matter, Darryl. They are still married, and she is still technically his wife. You never know what turnaround can happen. Marriages are weird like that."

Daniel had a point there.

"But damn bro, she's just right. Something about her, bro. I want her. I want her *bad*."

"Damn, I need to see this woman! I need to see who has my brother whipped like this!" Daniel laughed.

"Hey man, I'm *never* whipped. I just appreciate a woman in all her glory okay?!"

I had to laugh as well. Me, whipped! *HA!*

"Well man, I'll let you get back to bed. Don't want Jalisa to catch a case if she hears you whispering and laughing on the phone."

"Alright bro, I'll see you tomorrow at Sunday Dinner. Love ya!"

"Love you too bro, goodnight."

Chapter 8

D. Glove

April 2018

"Happy birthday to my baby brother! With each year that passes, I don't know how I still love and tolerate your punk ass!"

Daniel laughed, and so did the other guests.

"Nah, but in all seriousness, I just want to say that I love you, and there's nothing I wouldn't do for you. Let's make Chapter 35 the best one yet!"

We all raised our glasses and took a sip. Then the crowd started yelling *'Speech, Speech!'*

Daniel handed me the mic.

"I want to thank everyone for coming here tonight. It's a blessing to see 35 years of life, and I'm grateful for every moment of it. Also, I'm grateful for every person in this room. Each of you play a significant role in my life, and I couldn't be who I am without you."

I looked over at Tiffany with desire. She smiled and looked away.

"So, lets raise our glass again, and toast to life and happiness!"

We all raised our glass for another cheers.

"DJ, let's get it!"

The DJ kicked the music off again. I went around the room giving fists bumps to the fellas and hugging the ladies who came out to celebrate with me tonight. I then stepped outside for a minute of fresh air. I heard footsteps approaching behind me.

"Want to know a fun fact? Daddy said Mama almost named me Derek. Yet he wanted to go with his favorite actor Danny Glover. So, he chose Daniel. No wonder everybody at school called me Mister. Daddy wrong for that, huh?"

We laughed.

"Man, you tell me that same 'fun fact' every time we come to this hotel."

I turned around and saw Hotel Derek written on top of the hotel.

"I saw that look you gave Tiffany in there. She still curving you, huh?"

Daniel then pulled a blunt out of his pocket and lit it. He took a puff then passed it to me. I took a hit.

"Yea man. I don't know what it is. She continuously says that she is separated from her husband; and she's just waiting to be served with divorce papers. But it seems like she is still holding on. Granted, I know she was not the one who wanted it to end. But who would want to stay with a man like that?"

"How you know what kind of man he is?"

I took another hit.

"Man, we talk almost every day. We have gotten really close over these last six months. She lets me in on a lot of personal things."

"So, what do you think the holdup is?"

"I don't know. Many of times, I've dropped hints that I would like to take her out as more than friends or coworkers. But when I try to make a move; she pulls away. She blames it on work, but I know that's not the case. I catch them vibes man; I know she is feeling me. I just can't figure it out."

Daniel patted me on the back.

"It be like that sometimes bro. She is probably just playing hard to get. If her husband hurt her like she says he did; she is scared man. Her wall is up. You just have to be willing and patient enough if you really want her. You seem invested in her though."

I let out a sigh.

"I am man. I hate to admit it, but I'm really feeling this chick. And the part that makes me feel some type of way: is that I can't get her. Any woman I want, I get. It's crazy because all these other women be throwing themselves at me. And I don't even want them like that. But I *want* Tiffany. This shit messing my head up."

"Damn! Is this my baby brother I am talking to? Never heard you speak about a woman like that before. Are you okay in there?"

Daniel put his hand on my forehead as if he were checking my temperature. I smiled at his gesture.

"That wall will come down, and you will get her. Patience man, patience. If she is everything you expect her to be, she will be worth the wait."

Daniel then took the blunt away from me.

"Now give me back my blunt. I didn't come out here for you to smoke it all up; crying and shit."

We laughed. Daniel took a couple of more hits and put it out. We then started to head back inside.

"Man, Carmen has the best weed man. Me and Jalisa damn near getting high every weekend! Where does she get this shit from?"

I laughed and shrugged my shoulders.

"She won't reveal her sources man."

Daniel laughed.

"Man, the way Tiffany has you all in your feelings; let's be happy Carmen couldn't be here tonight. You still seeing her later tonight?"

"Yea, I'm headed that way when we leave here."

"Cool. Let her know we need some more of that good. Our stash is low."

"Alright, I'll let her know."

"Thanks. So, question. If you do end up dating Tiffany; how do you think she'll receive the relationship you and Carmen have?"

I shrugged my shoulders.

"I don't know man. I mean Carmen and I have a different type of relationship. She is a great, dear friend to me. Just one with benefits. It started off sexual, but now we are really close. I can talk to her about anything. I mean, we still have sex occasionally; but it's not all about that."

Daniel laughed.

"I can guarantee you that occasional, and 'great, dear friend' shit is not going to fly with a woman like Tiffany. If she comes from a relationship that she was getting cheated on in, I'm pretty sure she's not too fond of casual, lady friends. Just something to think about my brother."

Daniel then patted me on the back again.

"Okay, let's get back inside before your guests think they aren't appreciated."

1 Week Later

A week passed, and I returned to work from my birthday vacation. I walked into the studio and Tiffany was already in her booth. She greeted me with a wave as I walked towards her.

"Hey, can we talk tonight after the show?"

Tiffany smiled.

"Sure Daryl, about what?"

"You, me. I've been thinking about us—"

"Look Daryl, as much as I admire our friendship, I've told you before that I don't think this is a good idea. Respect my wishes, okay?"

I put my hands up as if I surrendered.

"I'll leave it alone."

I walked out of her booth and went back to my desk. I began setting my scene. Once everything was settled, I started my show:

"Alright, alright. It's Midnight Love, with ya boy D. Glove. Turning up this Houston heat, while you lay in your sheets. Giving you tunes so smooth, aiming to put you in the groove."

I looked over and winked at Tiffany.

"Tonight, I want to talk about love in the workplace. Houston, I

want to hear all about your hook ups at the job. How was it? Was it a booty call, did it work out, was it with your boss? I want to hear it all! Now let me play these jams to set your mood. Phone lines are open. Talk to me Houston!"

I began playing my first set of songs. I looked up at Tiffany, and she was staring me down. I knew she didn't want to hear this all night, but I wanted her to know that love in the workplace was possible.

"The Groove 96.2. Caller, what's your name?"

"Monica."

"Monica, you want to tell us about your experience with love in the workplace?"

"Yes, D. Glove. I had an encounter with my coworker. He was a much older coworker, but it seemed like he could keep up with a younger woman like myself."

"If you don't mind Monica; would you mind sharing y'all's ages?"

"I'm 24 and he's 48."

"20+ years huh, Monica? Now is this some sugar baby type of ordeal, or what?" I joked.

Monica laughed on the other end.

"Nah, not like that. It was my first job out of college, and I was assigned to him to learn the ropes of the company since he had been there for over 10 years. As we worked so closely together; we just got to know one another better. And we clicked. Fast forward to two years later, we're getting married next month!"

"Y'all are already engaged after two years of knowing each other? I see he snatched that PYT up quick!"

"Yep, he couldn't let me pass him by. He knew what he was doing." Monica laughed again.

"Well alright Monica! I'm not mad at y'all! Promise me one thing."

"What's that D. Glove?"

"Save me some cake and a dance at the wedding; I'm coming!"

Monica let out a laugh on the other end.

"We'll see you soon then!"

"You got it baby girl. Congratulations!"

"Thank you."

I then ended the call and looked up at Tiffany. Monica proved my point! Tiffany did not look impressed though. She rolled her eyes and looked away. My next caller was coming through.

"The Groove 96.2. Caller, what's your name?"

A male's voice came across the phone.

"I'd like to keep that anonymous for this story that I'm about to tell!"

I laughed.

"Man, this must be a good one."

The caller laughed back.

"Yea, D. Glove. I got a good one for you. I used to work for a nonprofit company that was owned by a husband and wife. I was putting in a lot of hours because the job was so difficult, you know. So, to make a long story short. One night I was working late while the husband was on vacation. Why his wife wasn't with him, I'm not sure. But anyway, at one point it was only me and the wife at the job. She came on to me, saying how she's been having her eyes on me since the interview. D. Glove, I laid her out all up and through that office!! We went from her office, to my office, to the file room, to the copy room; I mean we had sex everywhere!"

"You lucky devil, you! So, tell me man, what's up with you and the wife now?"

"Feelings got too strong, and I had to leave the job man. I quit. I thought I could be her boy toy, but things got too deep for me. I still see her frequently; but I just couldn't work under those conditions. I couldn't take seeing her all lovey-dovey with another man."

"Aww brother, I hope things work out for you in your love life. Keep your head up!"

"Thanks D. Glove."

I ended the call and looked back up at Tiffany. She said one word. "Exactly!" I was starting to wonder if this topic was a good idea.

We finished up the show with more calls and music. The responses were mixed, but it turned out to be a good show. Most of the callers agreed that love in the workplace was possible. Proving my point. I was hoping it was persuasive enough for Tiffany.

Tiffany and I packed up our belongings and started walking out to the parking garage. We waved goodnight to Mr. Freddy, and he waved back. He watched us walk to my car from the window and went back to securing the building. As soon as we were out of ear shot, Tiffany went in.

"That little stunt you pulled tonight wasn't cute. Just like that anonymous caller said: he had to leave his job because he got in too deep. I don't think you or I are willing to risk everything."

By this time, we made it to my car and got in. I drove around to the 5th floor to drop her off to her car. Our nightly routine. We made it to her car, and I put mine in park.

"But she was married and had obligations to another man. She had everything to lose."

"Just like *I* have everything to lose. You know my financial situation. I can't afford to lose this job." Tiffany said.

I continued on like she hadn't even said anything. I had to get these things off my chest.

"I'm able to not mix business with pleasure, Tiffany. If you want to stay private, we can be private. If you want to be public, we can be public. I just want to be with you in some type of way. I want you, Tiffany. I can't help the way I feel about you."

Tiffany shook her head.

"Plus, my divorce is not final. I have held out hope that he hasn't finalized it because there may still be a chance that we could work things out. I do not want to get you caught up in my mess. I know I must sound like a fool; but I still love him. I just want to be honest with you."

I wish this woman could see the worth I see in her instead of holding onto a man that treated her like shit.

"Tiffany; I can be better to you than your husband. I just wish that you give us a try. I am a big boy. I can keep my feelings in check. I could walk away if you chose to go back."

"It's more than keeping your feelings in check. Just trust me, Darryl. You do not want to get involved with me and my mess. I have to go now. I'll see you tomorrow."

Tiffany got out of the car and walked to hers. She got in and left rather quickly. I followed behind her to the bottom of the parking garage; and we then went our separate ways. Twenty minutes later, I received a text from her.

"Made it home."

I sent her the thumbs up emoji in return.

"That's all I get? Are you mad at me?"

"Not mad."

"Disappointed?"

"Not disappointed."

"So, you're going to be difficult with me?"

"Not being difficult."

"Okay, Darryl. I can see you do not want to talk. I will talk to you later then. Goodnight."

"Goodnight."

I was a bit frustrated with Tiffany. I'm getting tired of the cat and mouse game with her. I knew she wanted me and was playing hard to get. I shook those thoughts as I got home. I pulled into my garage and went inside. I showered, got comfortable, and called Carmen.

"Hey D. Calling me after your set. What's wrong? Or you want me to come over?"

"What's up Carmen. I just feel like talking."

"Tiffany giving you problems again?"

"Yea, I'm just frustrated with her. It's like I know she's feeling me, but she won't let herself go all the way."

"You have to give her time D. She just got out of a bad relationship with her husband. Feelings are still there, and obviously her emotions are all over the place. I actually feel bad for baby girl. I was her back in my younger days with my ex-husband Jim. I swore off men treating me like that and now I am who I am. But it takes time to get there, D. If she gives hints here and there that she is feeling you; trust me, I'm sure she is. She just has to figure out when the time is right for her."

I listened intently to what Carmen was saying and tried taking it to heart.

"Yea, yea. I hear you." Anyway, why you up so late? Want me to come over?"

"I had a long week with the new hires that just started. I'm about to roll up and watch television. You're more than welcome to stop by."

"Cool, see you in a few."

I hung up the phone and put my shoes on. I headed over to Carmen's house.

I made it to Carmen's house and unlocked the door. She had given me a key after countless trips back and forth. She didn't have a key to my place though. Said she did not need it; that she didn't want me to think she was too clingy. I did not fight her on that just in case things ever got out of hand.

Carmen was in her office and called out to me.

"I made you a drink D., it's on the kitchen counter. Seems like you need to relax."

I took a sip and exhaled a sigh of relief. She made it just how I like. Heavy on the Crown, light on the cranberry with a dash of lime. I sat down in the living room and surfed through the channels. Couldn't go wrong with The Fresh Prince of Bel-Air, so I turned it on. She then walked into the living room, rubbing on my shoulders from behind me.

"I hate to see you stressed like this D. Maybe if I told Tiffany how good you were in bed; she'd reconsider". She said in a joking manner.

"I just can't understand why I'm so caught up on this chick. And why it's bothering me so much that I can't have her."

Carmen then sat next to me.

"You're falling for her. When you really like someone in that way, it's hard to stop thinking about them. Hard to not want them more than they want you. But like I said before, you're going to have to give her time. She came from a really bad situation. Not everyone is ready to hop from man to man. Things like that takes a while."

"You're right."

I continued sipping my drink as Carmen and I laughed while watching The Fresh Prince of Bel-Air. Two episodes in, Carmen invited me upstairs to her bedroom where we capped off the rest of the night; pleasing each other.

I would rather be pleasing Tiffany, but hey, a man still has his needs.

Chapter 9

Tiffany

May 2018

Months had passed by since my separation from my husband, and surprisingly things were going pretty well. Lauren helped me find a nice place in the River Oaks area; just like I promised myself. I signed an 18-month lease for security. It felt empowering to have a job and a place of my own again.

I was meeting Lauren for brunch at one of our favorite spots, Upper Kirby Bistro. I walked into the restaurant, and Lauren waved at me to catch my eye. I walked over to her and sat down.

"What are you doing with these bags, girl? Did you go shopping without me?" She asked as I was sitting down.

"Just was out shopping, and thought I'd pick us up something."

I handed her three of the four bags I was carrying.

"I just wanted to thank you for all that you've done for me. We were practically strangers, and you let me into your home, rent free. And you hooked me up with a job making more money than I have ever made! I can't thank you enough!"

Lauren blushed.

"Aww thank you Tiffany. You didn't have to do this. I'm just happy I was fortunate enough and able to help a woman in need. And I enjoyed your company. I get bored in that condo by myself. Hell, sometimes I wish you'd come back!" We laughed with one another.

"Well, the gifts won't open themselves. Open them."

Lauren began opening up the gifts. Her face lit up with joy.

"The suit I've been wanting from Saks!! I was just about to buy it tomorrow!! Thank you so much Tiffany!" She gave me a hug.

"You're welcome. But keep looking; there's more bags!"

Lauren continued opening up the other bags. I also bought her shoes and a purse to match her suit. She checked out the purse, and saw it was filled with $2,500.

"Tiffany! You did not have to do this! I'm keeping the gifts, believe that, but take this money. I can't accept this from you." She said as she handed me the money.

I shook my head and handed her back the money.

"I know it's not much, but this is the least I could do. I would've spent way more paying rent for the eight months you let me stay with you. Please accept this as a gift from my heart."

Lauren blushed, grabbed my hand and held on to it.

"Thank you, Tiffany. I really appreciate the gesture and heartfelt thought."

I smiled back at her.

"You're welcome. Now let me see what I want to eat today."

Lauren and I browsed the menu while we sipped our mimosas. The waitress came over and took our orders.

"We'll have the Frenched Bone-in Porkchop and the Creole Salmon, ma'am."

The waitress repeated our order for clarity and said she would be back in a few with our food.

"So, let's get to planning this housewarming Tiffany. Have you thought of any dates?"

"Yes, I was looking at June 16th, that's not too close is it?"

"Nah, that should be a good enough time frame. So, we have about a month to plan. Who all did you want to invite?"

"My coworkers, some of my book club members, and some girls from the Kick Boxing class. Altogether, that's about 20 people, not including their spouses or plus ones."

"That sounds like a good amount of people. I will get started on the Evites tonight and they will be sent out by tomorrow."

"Thank you so much Lauren for your help."

"Sure girl, you know I got you."

Lauren and I continued discussing the housewarming party.

"So, what do you think about Darryl coming over? How do you think that is going to play out?"

"Ooh Lauren, I don't know. He has been coming on to me tough these past couple of weeks. He is not backing down."

"I don't know why you just don't give in. I know you still have some emotional ties to Calvin but that doesn't have anything to do with Darryl blowing your back out. Hell, we all need some TLC every once in a while."

"Yes, I can't lie. Sometimes I do sit there and fantasize about us having passionate sex. I just imagine his body all over me. His chocolate skin is so rich in melanin, I can't take it girl! And friend! When he comes in there smelling all good and get to talking sexual to the listeners! I have to zone out. Many of times I've had to excuse myself to the bathroom to release myself."

"See girl, Darryl could be doing that for you. You wouldn't have to lift a finger. *Literally*."

Lauren and I laughed out loud at the same time.

"I just don't know Lauren. I don't know if I should chance it. Darryl seems like he wants more than sex, he seems to want a relationship with me. And I'm just not ready for all that."

"So, you're not feeling him like that?"

"I'm feeling him, but I'm still caught up on my husband. I don't want to drag Darryl in all of my mess. It's too complicated at the moment."

"Friend, you need to let that go! I understand you're holding out hope for Calvin to come back. But what if he never does? Are you going to keep living your life on hold, in anticipation of him coming back around? Stop selling yourself short Tiff!"

"I can't help the way I feel, Lauren. I mean we have been together since I was a young girl."

"Only you know what you can handle. I just want my friend to stop pleasing herself and have someone do it for her!"

I laughed at Lauren.

"Me too friend, me too."

1 Month Later

A month had passed by, and my housewarming party was finally here. Lauren was already at my place, helping me set up and lay out the food. Guests were supposed to start arriving in 30 minutes. I had just enough time to run and get into my party clothes. Lauren came in the bathroom with me and helped me touch up my hair and makeup. Just as we were putting on the final touches, my doorbell rang.

I had shots for everyone to take as they walked in, so I grabbed the tray of drinks and went to the door. Guest started pouring in quickly; and everyone received their drink at the door. Soon after, Darryl showed up with a male and female. I saw him taking off her coat and hanging it in the coat closet. I rolled my eyes at the idea of it being his woman. I just know he didn't bring his woman into my home! What was he thinking?!

He hugged me upon seeing me.

"Hey Tiff. I want to introduce you to my brother Daniel and my sister in law Jalisa. They always following me everywhere I go."

We all laughed. I sighed in relief.

"Hi Daniel and Jalisa, nice to meet you both. I've heard so much about you guys."

Jalisa's face lit up. She went in for a hug.

"Tiffany, we've heard so much about you. It's so good to put a face with a name. You know, Darryl talks about you al—"

Darryl soon interrupted and hovered over Jalisa.

"Alright Jalisa. Don't get carried away now. Tiff, can we look around and see your new place, if you don't mind?"

"Sure, look away."

Darryl, Daniel and Jalisa then walked away, checking out my place. Lauren came over quickly.

"So, who'd he bring?"

"His brother and sister in law. Her face lit up when she greeted me. She was about to say something juicy, but Darryl cut her off."

"I'm sure you'll find out soon enough."

Lauren walked off, with some of our workout buddies and I went off to entertain some of my coworkers. Shortly after, we opened the gifts my guests brought for my home. I thanked everyone for their contributions to my new humble abode.

Lauren then broke out the games and more shots. People were really enjoying themselves drinking and mingling. I was happy to have a cool group of people here in my new place, having a good time. It made being in Houston not seem as lonely as it once did.

In the midst of playing games, I snuck off to my bedroom to use the bathroom. When I came out, Darryl was standing in the middle of my bedroom.

"Darryl, what are you doing in here?"

"I saw you sneak off in here and thought I could talk to you alone."

Darryl took a step closer, and he was moving really

sluggish. I could tell he had one too many drinks.

"Darryl, you're drunk. You lost at least 5 rounds of the questions game, so I know you're full."

Darryl tried to stand up straight.

"I'm not drunk."

"Come on Darryl, you're drunk. And plus, our coworkers might have seen you come back here."

I walked up to Darryl and tried to escort him out of the room. Darryl stepped to the side and grabbed my hand, pulling me closer to him.

"Tiffany, please. You know why I'm in here. I don't know why you keep avoiding this, avoiding me. I know I'm not the only one feeling this; the chemistry we have."

Darryl was so close to me; I could smell the liquor seeping through his lips. And I could feel the heat radiating off of his body.

I hate to admit it, but he was right. I couldn't deny the passion I had for him.

"Stop fighting me."

Darryl began rubbing his hands up and down my body. He went into kiss me. I kissed him back but quickly pulled away.

"Darryl, *stop*." I managed to say.

Darryl kept caressing my body, and now my body was starting to heat up with fire. Especially my panties.

"I don't think you want me to stop. But I will if you want me to. You want me to?"

Darryl started kissing me again, now touching my nipples through my dress. They hardened really quick. And that wasn't the only thing hardening. I felt him growing inside of his pants.

"I don't know if I'm ready for this, Darryl. And I don't know if you're ready for me." I managed to say in between his tongue down my throat.

"I'm ready for it. I'm ready for all of you baby."

In that moment, I let go. I kissed him so hard, and he kissed me with passion. He started backing me up until I reached the chaise in the corner. Darryl sat me down and got on his knees.

"God, I've been wanting to taste you since the moment I laid eyes on you. I just know you taste as good as you look."

Darryl began raising up my dress. I laid my head back, slid my body forward and was ready to fulfill his taste buds....

"Tiffany girl what's taking you so long? Guests are ab"

I looked up and Lauren was staring at me with her mouth open, while I'm sitting half naked with Darryl's head between my legs.

"Well, alrighty then. I'll see you out there." Lauren ran out of the room like she saw a ghost.

Gosh, I was so embarrassed.

"See Darryl, I knew we shouldn't have done this. That

could have been one of our coworkers. You have to go."

Darryl stood up.

"*We shouldn't have done this?* You weren't saying that a minute ago. I could wait until everyone leaves and come back. And we can finish what we started."

"We shouldn't have started it, Darryl. Please leave. And let's not speak of this again. This was a mistake."

Darryl had a confused look on his face.

"It's not a mistake to me, Tiff. You know how I feel about you. I know what has happened to you, and I won't hurt you like that. I'm not your husband, stop pushing me away because of him."

He then became frustrated, and I could tell the liquor was speaking for him.

"You're only hurting yourself. I'm trying to help you out of this rut, but you make it so hard Tiffany! Goddamn!"

I then got irritated and became angry. Who did he think he was to tell me how I felt or should feel?

"So, you think I want to be hurt? You don't know what the fuck you're talking about! You don't know shit about my pain! And I'm not asking you to help me out of shit! I wouldn't have told you shit if I would've known you'd throw it back up in my face!"

I tried to calm myself down before people could hear me. But I was already on a roll and continued on.

"You don't think people talk?! I hear all about how you mess around with women all across this city. Yea, I've heard it all! You're probably worse than my husband! Get the fuck out my face, Darryl!"

Darryl opened his mouth but stopped himself. He then did as he was told and left, storming out of my room.

Shortly after, Lauren came back in the room.

"I'm sorry girl. I did not mean to interrupt y'all like that. It's just that guests were getting ready to leave and wanted to say goodbye to you before they left."

"No, it's okay. We needed to be stopped anyway."

I fixed myself up and walked out of the room to thank everyone and see them off. As I was getting closer to the living room, I saw Darryl, his brother and sister in law walking out of the door. I proceeded on to saying goodbye to everyone.

Once everyone was gone, Lauren began helping me clean up.

"So, girl, give me the details. From the looks of it, Darryl's head was going straight in between your legs! Y'all gonna finish what y'all started?" Lauren's eyes were lit up with excitement.

"No, I'm glad you walked in when you did. I almost gave in. Almost gave it to him."

"And remind me again why that would be a bad thing?"

"Besides the obvious; he made me upset. Tried telling me

that I need to let him help me get out of the rut I'm in. I don't need help with shit. I'm good. And plus, we work together. I don't need that drama at work."

"Girl, it's 2018. Nobody at work worrying about y'all messing around. And you're scared to be with someone. You can miss me with that 'he made me upset' crap. You're just creating another reason to distance yourself from happiness. That man knows everything about you and Calvin, and he is still willing to be with you. Admit it, you're scared."

"Okay, okay. Yes, I'm afraid Lauren. I'm entitled to being afraid, okay? I've been through a lot. I want to date again, but I'm afraid of being hurt again."

I walked off to the other side of the room. Tears began dropping down my face.

"I'm sorry Tiffany. I didn't mean to sound harsh. Yes, you have been through a lot and you have every right to be afraid. I just hate seeing you suffer for Calvin. He clearly has moved on with his life; and I just hate that you're not able to. I hate that he gets to have his cake and eat it too; while you suffer and neglect yourself."

Lauren walked over to me and hugged me.

"I'm sorry friend. Let it out. I'm here for you."

I sobbed on Lauren's shoulder while she hugged me. Here I was again. Sobbing on Lauren's shoulder; over Calvin. I have not heard or seen him in months; and he still had a hold on me. He still brought me heartache. When will this ever end?

Chapter 10

Darryl

June 2018

A week had passed, and things had been awkward with Tiffany at work. I gave her the space that she wanted and didn't bring up the night of her housewarming party; like she asked. We even stopped walking to our cars together at night. I did stick around to make sure that she left the garage safely though. As frustrated as I was with her, I still had to look out for her.

We began wrapping up our shift and at about 12:15AM. I played a 90's R&B love jams mix to carry out the next fifteen minutes. I started packing up my things, getting ready to go.

"Wait, Darryl. Can we talk, please?" Tiffany said as she burst out of her office.

I put my bag down and leaned up against my desk.

"Sure Tiff. Talk."

She walked over to the windows and closed all the blinds. She stood at the corner window with her back turned to me.

"I'm sorry for how I have been acting towards you. I have been playing with your feelings, and I was wrong for doing that. Yes, my husband hurt me something awful. And I'm afraid to be hurt again."

She turned around and tears were rolling down her face. All the frustration I built up for her over this past week instantly vanished. I walked over to her and held her hands.

"I have listened to you very well, and I've watched you cry many times. I wouldn't hurt you like that Tiffany."

"But my head is so screwed up Darryl. What if my husband comes back and wants to work it out? Then what? I don't want to hurt you."

"Then we will cross that bridge if or when we get to it. I'm a grown man. I can handle it."

"I just want to be honest and open with you Darryl. I still have feelings for him. I'm just—"

I cut her off.

"And *I* have feelings for you, Tiffany."

"Listen to me, Darryl. I'm not sure if I'm ready to jump into anything serious right now."

"Look, Tiffany. I do not care if you want anything serious with me or not. I just want to be with you. I want to be around you, in your presence outside of these walls. More than just a work event. I want to make you happy. I want to make you smile. I want to make you feel appreciated. I want to please you. *I just want you, Tiffany.*"

"Don't make me regret this, Darryl."

"I promise, I won't". I ensured her as I wiped a tear from her eye.

Tiffany locked the door, and then turned back to me. She began kissing me. She wrapped her arms around my neck and leaned in so close, our bodies felt intertwined. I held her around her waist and kissed her so passionately. We backed up to my desk and I sat her down. She helped me out of my shirt; and I helped her out of her pants. Everything was going so fast but seemed like we were going in slow motion. And I was enjoying every moment. She raised her own shirt and stood there staring at me. I took a step back and gawked over her body. I always dreamed of how she would look out of those clothes. Her body was better than what I could have imagined. *Better than I dreamed of.*

I began kissing her again and focused on getting her out of her bra and panties. I slid down her panties and freed her from them. I got down on my knees and sat her up on my desk. I then spread her legs wide eagle. I kissed and licked continuously at her flesh. She tasted amazing! *Better than I dreamed of.* She positioned herself with both of her legs on my back and grabbed the back of my head. She moaned and purred like a kitten. I continued feasting, spelling my name with my tongue. Stamping my name on her. Claiming and marking my territory. She was mine now. This kitty belonged to me.

Soon enough I heard those four magic words.

"I'm. About. To. Cum!"

Tiffany started thrusting her body back and forth on my face.

"Darryl, baby!"

Instantly, Tiffany's body felt like it was shocked with electricity. I felt her jerking on my face. I looked up and watched as ecstasy was written all over her face.

I wiped my face and then stood up. I pulled my pants down, ready to enter her. But Tiffany had other plans. She sat me down in the chair to taste me. She got on *her* knees and inhaled me with her mouth. She moaned and hummed on me as if she were singing a sweet tune. I grabbed a head full of her hair and threw my head back. I waited so long to feel her plump, juicy lips on me. I looked down at her and it was as if she was enjoying her favorite popsicle. I didn't mind being her sweet treat.

Shortly after, I felt it coming.

"I'm. About. To. Cum."

Tiffany covered me with her hand as I erupted into it. She then wiped her hand with the Kleenex on my desk. She backed up and leaned on my desk, waiting for me to join her. I walked up to her and slid myself inside of her. I instantly let out a soft moan. We got our groove and rhythm going. She wrapped her legs around my waist as I cupped her ass. She felt so good. *Better than what I dreamed of.* Everything was better than what I had dreamed it would be! I kept my pace slow and steady, stroking every inch of me into her body.

"Wait a minute. Back up baby." Tiffany instructed.

I backed up as I was told.

Tiffany turned around and bent over across my desk. I aligned myself with her body and entered her from the back.

"Ooh Tiffany, baby."

I poured into her. Gave her everything I had. This moment was finally here, and I wanted her to feel every part of me. Every stroke was everything I have been wanting to feel for so long. Her kitty was so wet, so tender, so perfect. She reached out and held on to the edge of the desk. I covered her hands with mines. I wanted her to feel protected. I wanted her to feel safe. I wanted her to know I would take care of her. I looked down and watched as my body sent waves through hers. I watched as her ass had ripple effects when it slapped back against mines. Her juices began to cover me. Then she said those four magic words again.

"*I'm. About. To. Cum!*"

She started moaning uncontrollably.

"Shh, baby. Someone might hear us."

She lowered her voice.

"Cum with me Darryl!" She said with a sweet whisper.

I grabbed her hips and drilled into her. And then, we came. Simultaneously. Both of us quietly letting out our moans. We then started breathing rugged; trying to catch our breath. I felt her body vibrating and pulsating. I stood there for a while, standing tall inside of her. Taking in what just happened. After a while she finally broke her silence.

"Damn, I really needed that Darryl. You felt so good inside of me."

I reached for a Kleenex off my desk.

"Anytime you need it, it's here for you Tiff."

I wiped her off first, and then wiped myself off. Tiffany struggled to stand up fully, but finally came to her feet. She asked for me to reach her clothes and shoes, which were tossed around my desk area. I picked them up and handed them to her. We both fixed ourselves up; making sure we looked presentable and the office looked normal. Tiffany went around the room, re-opening the blinds she previously closed.

"Darryl, can we keep this between us please? I don't want anyone to know."

"As long as you don't keep away from me."

Tiffany smiled and winked at me. We then unlocked the studio and headed out to the garage. We did our nightly routine. I drove her to her car, and before she got out; we held a long passionate kiss. She held my face with such tenderness.

"See you later, D."

She then got out of my car, got into hers, started it, and began driving down the garage. I followed behind her and watched her drive out.

On the way home, I rode in silence. Reminiscing about what just took place. The way she looked naked, the way she tasted, the sounds she made, the way her body tightened on mines. It scared me a little to know how hard I was falling for her.

When I pulled into my driveway, I heard a notification and picked up my phone. It was a text from Tiffany.

"Made it inside. Thank you for tonight. I can't wait for Round 2."

I smiled at my phone, while texting her back.

"Just made it home myself."

I then went inside. I walked into my bathroom and showered. I came out to the living room and sat in my recliner. I looked around my home and saw the same image. A lonely, cold home. Before I knew it, I was grabbing my keys from off the counter and heading back out to my car. I found myself driving over to Tiffany's house.

I text her when I arrived outside.

"Hey."

I wanted to see if she was still up. If not, I was going to

be ringing that doorbell. Quickly I saw the three bubbles pop up; letting me know she was typing.

"Hey, D. Did you make it home?"

"To your home, yes."

"What do you mean?"

"Open the door."

I got out of my car and walked up to her door. She opened up the door shortly after.

"You said you couldn't wait for Round 2. Neither could I."

I woke up the next morning in my bed, with a smile on my face. I had a chance to experience ecstasy with Tiffany twice in one night. I wished I could have stayed over at her house, but I chose to go home. I didn't want to come off too strong or overcrowd her space too soon. She wanted to take things slow, so I gave her the space she desired.

After getting dressed and eating breakfast, I headed over to Daniel's house to pick him up. We were going to shoot some hoops. I also wanted to fill him in on my night with Tiffany.

We arrived at the park and started shooting the ball around.

"What's going on in your world, big brother?" I said as I threw up some shots.

"Ahh, nothing to it. Jalisa and I had date night last night. Went to the movies to see Uncle Drew. Rather good movie. What about you?"

I thought he would never ask.

"Guess."

"Guess what?"

"Guess what I did last night? Better yet, guess who I did last night?" I said with a smile on my face.

He looked at me and raised his eyebrow. He then started laughing and raised his hand for a high five.

"My man! You finally got Tiffany? How'd you do it?"

"It was tough man, but I broke her down. I ain't even gone lie, I was in there begging like Keith Sweat." We both burst out laughing.

"You remember she had been acting funny with me since the housewarming, right? Well, we had been dodging each other since. We were on some real awkward shit. So last night when I was leaving, she stopped me saying she wanted to talk. She got to explaining herself; why she's been acting the way she's been acting. But to make a long story short, one thing led to another and we hit it off. Right there in the studio, on my desk. It was worth the wait, man. The girl knows what she's doing!"

Daniel laughed.

"My brother." He said as he fist bumped me. "So, what

did she say afterwards?"

"She told me how much she enjoyed it and needed it. And asked me to keep it private. We left, shared a passionate kiss in my car, and then went home. I was fiending for some more, so I drove my ass over to her house for another round. I left and went home though to give her some space. Didn't want to overwhelm her, you know?"

Daniel was standing there, cheesing. Which in turn made me laugh. We both stood there grinning; looking like two high school boys sharing stories of how we lost our virginity.

"Look at you! I am happy for you. But wait. What are you going to do about Carmen?"

"I'm going to let her know we have to stop sleeping with each other. I am sure she will understand. She is still my friend though. I don't want to lose her friendship. Just have to chill on the sex."

"Cool, cool. Well, I am glad you finally got your girl. I really like Tiffany. She is different than any other woman you've ever dated. She has class, easy to get along with, and she is down to earth. Plus, I can tell she likes you for you. Not for the status you have around Houston, or what you can do for her. I must say, though. Be careful with her still having feelings for her husband. That is a tricky game you are playing, bro. I know you think you can walk away when you want to. But once consistent sex starts, and your spirits get intertwined; feelings get deeply involved. And it is hard to turn that switch off. It's not as easy as you think. I don't want to get all Dr. Phil on you, but I gotta look out for you. You understand me, little bro?"

"Yes, I understand."

I took what Daniel said to heart. But I was already deeply involved. The feelings were there. It was way past sex for me. No turning back now. I would just have to face that situation if it happened.

Chapter 11

Tiffany

June 2018

I walked out of the gym and waited on Lauren to finish talking with some new Kick Boxing members. She walked out shortly, and we started walking over to the nearby park for a walk.

"Girl! I have been dying to hear this story!! I want all the juicy details!"

I laughed at her excitement.

"It was amazing Lauren! You know we hadn't talked for some time, and I really missed our friendship. Girl he was about to walk out the door, and I can't lie, I bolted out of there to stop him!" We both burst out with laughter.

"I asked if we could talk. He said okay. And I just really explained myself to him. Told him how sorry I was for my behavior, and so on and so forth. He forgave me, and one thing led to another. We got to kissing and clothes went to flying everywhere. I looked down and he was hung like a horse!"

"He was giving you baby leg vibes, girl??" Again, we burst out into laughter.

"Yes Lauren! A tree in his pants, okay! But the best part was that he was so passionate with me. He made it so comfortable to be with him. He's the only person I've been with outside of Calvin. I was so nervous about it. But he took care of that. It felt so good to receive some good loving. Some TLC that I haven't received in a long time."

I stopped to think about it.

"Damn girl; sounds mesmerizing. You sure you're not falling for him?"

"I don't know Lauren. I really don't know how I feel at this moment."

"Take your time, friend. There is no rush. Just don't wait too long and let him get away. He seems like a good catch. He's handsome, has a successful career, and is really into you. I know Calvin messed you up in the head; but don't make Darryl pay for Calvin's mistakes."

I really took in Lauren's words. She had a great point.

We then stretched and continued our walk on the track.

1 Week Later

I was on Briar Forest, driving over to Darryl's house. All

week he'd been telling me he had something special planned for me. Things had been going really smooth with him, and I appreciated that.

I arrived at his home and got out of my car. I grabbed my overnight bag from the trunk and went up to the door. I knocked and he answered shortly. I could see that he still needed time to get dressed.

"And women are the ones always getting called out for needing more time."

"Yea, yea. I'll be quick. My brother called and held me up a little bit."

Darryl went off to his bedroom to finish getting dressed. I walked around his home, appreciating the photos and artwork he had. I came across a picture of him and his family. Then a picture of him and his brother. I stared at it, admiring their relationship. Wishing I had the same with my sister. He came out and saw me staring and holding the picture.

"You going to leave me for my brother, or something? You're staring way too hard at him." He joked.

"Nah. Just admiring the bond you and you brother have. Sometimes I wish my sister and I could push past our differences."

"I'm sorry to hear that. Have one of y'all tried reaching out to one another recently?"

I sighed. "No, I know she doesn't want to talk to me. I've

tried calling her numerous times but gave up on it after a while. She cut me off. I've accepted it."

"You never know. Don't give up hope."

I sighed again. "Enough about that though. Are you ready to go?"

"Sure am. Let's roll."

Darryl escorted me out and opened my car door. We drove downtown and pulled up at Vic & Anthony's.

"Aww Darryl. You brought me to Vic & Anthony's? How'd you know I wanted to come here?"

"I overheard you telling Lauren a few times how much you wanted to check this place out."

"That's so sweet of you babe." I gave him a quick peck on the lips.

We got out of the car, and Darryl turned the keys over to the valet. The restaurant was a nice romantic place. Our hostess greeted us and took us to a private room. We walked into the room, and a band was playing soft jazz in the rear corner. The room was decorated with fresh floral arrangements: red and white roses. White roses and candles filled our dining table as the centerpiece.

"Enjoy your dinner, ma'am and Mr. Glover." The hostess said before leaving the room.

I wrapped my arm around him. "Ooh this is beautiful, *Mr. Glover.*"

"Hey, being a local celeb has it's perks." Darryl joked.

"I can't believe you did all of this for me."

"Why wouldn't I? Aren't you deserving of it?"

I nodded my head in agreement and smiled. Yes. Yes, I am deserving of this.

A waiter was standing at our table. He introduced himself as he pulled back my seat and helped me get tucked in. He then poured us a glass of wine. My favorite, Cabernet. He laid the menu down on the table and said he would give us a few minutes. He walked away and closed the door behind him.

"Darryl, you really went out of your way tonight. Thank you. I really appreciate it."

"You're welcome. You've been through a lot and I thought you could use someone appreciating you."

Darryl was right. I needed to let go of all my baggage, and just enjoy the space I'm currently in.

After going over the menu, the waiter returned, and we ordered. The waiter took our orders and left the room again. He came back with our first course of the night. We dined, sipped our wine and talked some more. He told me about a BBQ his family was having at his brother's house for the Fourth of July. He asked me to come and I agreed. I was nervous to meet his family but couldn't wait.

Our waiter came back with our main course, and we continued talking, enjoying our fine cuisine and sipping wine.

After finishing our meal, he asked for my hand and walked me to the middle of the floor for a dance.

Darryl placed his arms around my body. I embraced him, laying my head on his chest. We began to dance, our bodies joining as one. We swayed back and forth, listening to the smooth tunes

"I want you to know I'm for real about us, Tiffany. I know I can't change what happened to you in the past, but I hope to give you a better future. Make you feel appreciated. Make you feel desired."

I was so wrapped up; all I could mumble was "Thank you."

I closed my eyes and took in this moment. Darryl made me feel important. He treated me with such care and compassion. The more we swayed back and forth, I grew hot for him. The waiter came back, and I asked for the check.

"We still haven't had dessert baby."

"The way I'm feeling right now, you are my dessert."

"You don't have to tell me twice."

Darryl handed the waiter $300. "Keep the change, brother."

He patted the waiter on the back, tipped the musicians, thanked them all for the lovely dinner, and we then left out of the room. We waited for his car at Valet, and it finally arrived. We got in the car and headed out to Darryl's place.

The heat I felt inside of me wasn't going to let me make it to his house though. I needed a quickie right now before I drenched his front seat. I asked him to pull over on a deserted side street. He did as told.

"Turn the car off, take your pants off, and lay your seat back."

Darryl followed my instructions. I slid my panties off and hiked up my dress. I got on top of him and straddled him. I began kissing him. I felt him growing under me. I slid him inside of me, and a soft moan escaped me. I got my rhythm going and started riding him. He cupped my ass and threw his head back. He felt so good inside of me. I wanted to make this feeling last a while, but a quickie was all I could get on this downtown street. I picked up my pace. He grabbed my hips and guided me into a nice groove. We stayed at this pace for a while, listening to Tank sing "When We" over the radio. I looked into his eyes and could feel his desire and passion staring back at me. Our patchy breathing aligned with one another as we continued this quick but satisfying escapade. Every intimate moment with him was always intense. I felt ways about Darryl that I never felt before.

"I'm. About. To. Cum. Tiffany!" He said as his eyes rolled to the back of his head.

My breathing became faster as I was also feeling myself reaching climax. I then felt him releasing his heat inside of me.

"Oh, shiiiiiit baby." Darryl said as he came.

My body started to buckle as I came also.

We started tongue kissing. So passionately. I pulled back from him as I heard people laughing and talking loudly. I looked up and saw some party goers at the top of the street, crossing over and walking in the direction of the car.

"Oh, shit. We are about to have company soon. We gotta get out of here before they see us."

I quickly got off him and hopped back into my seat. We wiped ourselves, fixed our clothes, and soon drove off. Once we got back on Hwy 59, we both burst out laughing at the thought of getting caught by a group of 18-year-olds.

Chapter 12

Tiffany

September 2018

A few months passed by, and things have been going great with Darryl. I finally was in a space again where I felt happy with myself. Darryl made that easy for me. He spoiled me and made it perfectly clear that he wanted me and only me.

My birthday was today, and I reflected on my life in the past year. This time last year, I was sleeping on Lauren's couch, jobless, and heartbroken. This year, I had my own place, worked at Houston's top R&B station, and was happy in my relationship. I started to cry. And this year, I was crying tears of joy.

I was in the middle of doing my makeup when I heard a knock at the door. I opened it and was greeted by a bouquet of roses. The delivery guy handed me the bouquet and card.

"Have a wonderful birthday, ma'am."

I took the flowers and thanked him. But before he made it to his van, an Edible Arrangement van pulled up. I put the flowers down and ran back to the door to meet the woman bringing me the fruit package.

"Okay, ma'am! Somebody loves you; I see! Get it, girl! Happy Birthday!"

I laughed at her candid, playful reaction.

"Thank you, sis!"

She smiled and walked away. I shut the door behind me and placed the Edible Arrangement on the counter next to the roses. I pulled out the card and read it.

"Tiffany, I never would have imagined that you would come into my life and shake it up the way you did. Before you, I never wanted to be in a committed relationship. I was able to have my cake and eat it too. But now, the only cake I want is you. I know what happened to you around this time last year. I hope to make you forget it even happened. Can't wait to see you later tonight.

Love, Darryl"

I called Darryl and thanked him for my card, flowers and fruit arrangement. He let me know that it was his pleasure.

I placed the flowers on the coffee table and brought the fruit with me to the living room. I started nibbling on a few pieces. My phone had been going off all morning from various people calling me. I held out hope for Tracy calling me; but she never did. It hurt me a little, but I told myself I would not spend another birthday crying over anyone.

I checked my phone again and Lauren texted me saying she was on her way. I went back in the bedroom to finish my makeup and slip my outfit on.

Lauren, Jalisa, and some of my workout buddies were helping me celebrate by going out to brunch, and then bar hopping in the Heights.

Lauren arrived shortly after.

"Hey friend! Happy 30th birthday!" Lauren screamed with excitement.

"Thank you, friend!!"

"First and foremost, we need birthday shots. I brought your favorite."

She pulled out a small bottle of Crown Apple.

"It's barely noon girl, and you turned up!"

"Yea, yea. It's 5 o'clock somewhere. Go get us some shot glasses!"

I walked into the kitchen and came back with two shot glasses. She poured us our shots.

"On the count of 3. You ready?"

I nodded my head yes.

"1. 2. 3!"

We both took our shot.

"Alright girl, it's time to turn up! Let's roll."

I grabbed my purse and we headed out. We met up with the other girls and got the festivities rolling.

After enough partying, eating, and drinking; Lauren dropped me off back home so I could get ready for my birthday dinner with Darryl at Steak 48. It was my first time, and I was excited to go. Darryl was coming to pick me up at 7:30PM. I looked over at the clock and it was 5:28PM. I knew I wanted to look damn near perfect tonight, so I figured I would redo my makeup and hair. I showered again and started start getting ready.

At about 7:25PM, Darryl was knocking on the door. I opened it, expecting a big reaction. Because I know I look damn good!

"Damn baby, you look stunning! I mean, you always look good, but wow!"

I did a spin around for him, blushing at his compliments.

"I worked all evening on my hair and makeup. I'm glad you like it."

"I love it!"

He leaned in and gave me a quick peck on the lips. He reached out for my hand as I locked up. He then escorted me to the car. He opened my door first allowing me to get in then headed around to the driver side and opened his. He got in and we headed off to the restaurant.

We arrived at the restaurant shortly after and were greeted by the hostess who then escorted us to our table. We started off with wine and appetizers, and then moved onto the main course. After we finished dinner, we waited around for dessert. Upon waiting, he pulled out my birthday gift from his jacket pocket. It was an envelope adorned with a bow.

"Aww, baby! Thank you! Ooh, what could this be in an envelope?"

I opened the gift, and it was two plane tickets to Montgomery and a hotel conformation. They were scheduled for the Christmas Holiday. I hadn't been home since my last encounter when Tracy ignored me. Which was over a year ago. I looked at him with a confused look on my face.

"Hear me out. I know how much your relationship with your sister means to you. I am not sure if you had any holiday plans, but I figured that Christmas would be a good time to take a trip home. Holiday season always bring out the best in people. She won't be able to ignore or dodge you at Christmas dinner, right?" He said with a smile on his face.

I could not believe that he had enough thought and care to help mend the relationship between me and Tracy. My emotions took over me, and I covered my face with my hands and began crying hard. He reached over and grabbed my hands.

"Am I overstepping my boundaries? I'm sorry, I didn't mean to make you cry."

"No, that's really sweet of you. I wasn't expecting this at all. Thank you so much, honey."

"You're welcome. I'm hoping for the best between y'all."

"I can't believe this. Thanks again baby. Mending my relationship with my sister would be the best gift ever!"

I gave him a kiss and a long hug. Who knew letting go of Calvin would turn out like this?

We finished up at the restaurant and headed back to my place. We capped off the night with Cabernet and amazing birthday sex.

Happy birthday to me!

Chapter 13

Tiffany- Montgomery, AL

Christmas Eve 2018

Darryl and I arrived in Montgomery two days ago. I called my mother the day after I received the tickets from Darryl to set up my plans. I convinced her not to tell Tracy I was coming home. She was reluctant at first, but finally gave in. I was too afraid that Tracy would avoid me again.

These past few months I have been really nervous about this trip. But it was finally here. I really wanted to talk to Tracy and fix our relationship. If it wasn't for meeting Lauren, I don't know what I would have done when Calvin left me. Tracy was the only other person I could talk to. As much as we feuded with each other; she was not only my sister, she was my best friend.

I was happy to share with her that Calvin and I were finally separated and that I moved on and met someone new.

I know that news alone will at least make her want to talk to me.

Darryl and I were having breakfast inside the hotel. After breakfast, I was going over to my parents to finally have this conversation. Every Christmas Eve, Tracy and I would go over to help my mother prepare the Christmas dinner food so I knew I would find her there for sure.

I finished up breakfast with Darryl and kissed him goodbye. He was going to go shopping for some gifts at the mall while I was with my family.

I arrived at my parents' house and saw that Tracy was already there. I parked my car and started walking up to the door. I could smell the food as I got closer. If nothing else went right, at least I would have my mother's good cooking that I hadn't had for over a year. As I put my key in and turned the knob, I braced myself. I walked in and could hear Tracy in the middle of a conversation.

"Hey Mama. Hey, Tracy." I said as if this was a regular encounter.

Tracy stopped talking in mid conversation. I knew she recognized my voice. I walked into the kitchen where they were, and Tracy looked like she saw a ghost. Then she looked disgusted. There was a brief moment of awkward silence; before Mama broke the ice.

"Hey, my baby. I'm so happy you're with us this year for

Christmas."

My mama came up and hugged me. I hugged her back.

"Tracy, don't you want to say hello to your sister? You haven't seen her in a while."

Tracy stood there, folded her arms, and rolled her eyes. I reached out my arms for a hug. Tracy did not budge.

"Really Tracy? It's been almost two years. How stubborn can you be?"

"I can be what I want to be. You know what, I'm out of here!" Tracy tried walking away.

"Stay your ass right there and don't you dare move!" Mama yelled out.

"Now, I have tried to stay out of y'all business. But I'm sick of you girls fighting like cats and dogs. Y'all been like this all your lives, and it's going to stop today. Tracy, you have taken this too far. Your sister flew all the way here just to talk to you. She came here last year, and you ignored her. You will not ruin this holiday for us. Go upstairs, talk to Tiffany; and work this out! And I am not going to say it again!"

"Alright mama, damn! You don't have to yell!"

"Curse at me again and see what happens." My mama said as she raised her hand, as if she was going to slap Tracy.

"Sorry, Mama."

Tracy walked past me and walked towards the stairs. I followed behind her, and we walked into her old room.

"What's up, Tiffany? What do you want?" Tracy said as she folded her arms and leaned up against the dresser.

"Don't be like that, Tracy. It's been too long. Can we work this out?"

"Oh, I'm sorry. Your hoe of a sister has been too occupied out here fucking and sucking everything that walks. I guess I didn't have time to work it out."

"I shouldn't have said that to you, and I apologize."

"You're damn right you shouldn't have said those things. That's how you really feel about me? That I'm a hoe? A slut? That hurts Tiffany. I couldn't believe you said those things about me."

I came here with the intent of being transparent and honest with Tracy. I was ready to put this behind me. The words damn near fell out of my mouth.

"I don't think you're a hoe. I actually admire how you're able to move on so quickly and don't get too invested in a man. Or let a man get the best of you and your feelings. I did and look what happened to me. I am sorry for the things I said and how I reacted that night. But Tracy, you've said some hurtful things to me over the years as well. And I've let it slide because I know Calvin has done some foul things. But you have to watch how you talk to me as well."

Tracy stared off into space. I don't know if anything I was saying was getting through to her. So, I kept trying.

"Tracy, I love you and I want our relationship to get better. We are family Tracy; and you can't choose your family. But we can choose how we treat one another. We've always had a rocky relationship; but it doesn't have to be that way. The only way for us to get better is to try. We have to be willing to make the change. And I'm choosing to make things work and be better between us. I hope you will try as well."

Tracy opened her mouth, but soon paused. I knew she was about to say something smart. But what she said next surprised me.

"I've been acting like a bitch, and I have to do better. I can admit that. I have had time to think, and I shouldn't have distanced myself from you. It was childish and petty of me. I'm sorry for all of the things I've said to you as well. I was out of line and should have respected your decisions for your relationship. I love you too, and I'm willing to make the change for us to be better also."

I reached out for a hug, and Tracy embraced me.

"I have to say this though, Tiffany. I love you and I want the best for you. I hate the fact that Calvin has treated you with disrespect over the years, and that is where my anger came from. But it never had anything to do with me hating you. I just want the top of the line for you. You deserve so much more."

"Well, just so you know. Calvin and I are no longer

together. I got a new man now!"

Tracy's face lit up with excitement.

"Shut the front door! How did this happen? When did this happen?"

"Well, come to find out, that bitch you caught him with actually lives in Houston. She works at the news station with him as a meteorologist. Her name is Tabitha Dixon."

"Are you kidding me? How did you find out?"

"During Hurricane Harvey. I was watching the news coverage on the hurricane, and she just appeared right there in my face. Reporting live about the expected weather."

"Are you serious? Shut up!"

"Nope, I couldn't believe it either. Well, I called and called Calvin, and he never answered or came home for two weeks. He was with her the whole time."

"So, you mean to tell me he was with her for those two weeks? And not his wife?"

"Yep, the whole city was flooded and there was nowhere to go. The news crew were set up and stayed at the hotel. Which means he was with her at the hotel for two weeks, while I was all alone scared to death of the possibility of being flooded out."

"Oh my god, Tracy."

"That's not even the worst part. When the sun finally came out and the flooding stopped, I went out with my friend.

I guess he saw it as his opportunity to come back to the house and get some things. And had the nerve to come back with her. I caught him on the cameras and hauled ass back to the house. And I kicked both they ass!"

"Just like big sis taught you!" Tracy laughed and gave me a high five.

"Yep, just like you taught me." I laughed and high fived her back.

"So, what else happened?"

"Well, he went off on me, and finally showed his true colors. He basically told me he was leaving me for her, and that I had a week to move out. So, I moved out and in with my friend. Until I found a steady job working as an engineer at the radio station."

"I'm so sorry Tiffany. I really feel horrible now. I wish I could've been there for you."

"That's water under the bridge now."

"Well, tell me about this new man!"

Tracy and I caught up for the next hour.

It was good to settle my differences with her. Who knew that a simple, yet vulnerable conversation could be so meaningful? I hoped that we could keep this same energy between us. I was tired of fighting my sister. I just wanted peace in my life from here on out. We walked out of the room and found Mama sitting outside the room in the rocking chair on the landing.

"Mama, were you there the whole time?" Tracy asked.

"I sure was. Had to make sure you girls didn't kill each other. Then who's going to help me finish peeling these sweet potatoes for my pies?" We all laughed and hugged each other.

"I'm so happy to be home with my family. I've missed y'all so much. I'm also happy for you all to meet Darryl tomorrow."

After Tracy and I finished helping Mama prepare everything, we parted ways until the next day. On my way back to the hotel, I called Darryl because I couldn't wait to tell him how great things went. I had to tell him now. I could tell through his voice that he was excited and happy for me. I arrived back at the hotel and walked into the room.

Darryl had it decked out with roses, candles, and wine. He greeted me at the door with a kiss and was dressed in a robe and boxers. I looked over and saw presents wrapped in the corner of the room.

"Someone has been busy today, I see."

"Yes, I wanted to make this a special Christmas for you. I went out and bought some presents for your little cousins. I also bought some gifts for your sister and parents. And I bought this for you."

Darryl pulled out Christmas themed lingerie.

"You can get your other gifts tomorrow, but I want you

to get this one tonight."

Darryl walked to the mini fridge and pulled out a bottle of Cabernet. He poured a glass and asked me to take it to the bathroom. I went into the bathroom and noticed that he drew me a bubble bath.

"Aww baby, this was so sweet of you."

I quickly undressed and got into the tub while the water was still hot. He came in and turned on the jets.

"I want you to relax and come out of here when you're ready. I'll be waiting on you."

Darryl placed the lingerie on the counter.

"Model that for me when you get out."

He then walked out of the bathroom and shut the door behind him. I heard him turn the television on to a sports channel. For a moment, I laid in the tub and shed a single tear. I felt so lucky to have a man take care of me and show concern for me. I felt appreciated, respected, and wanted. Something I wanted to feel in my marriage that I haven't felt in a long time. I deserved this happiness. I deserved this man.

After relaxing and soaking, I finally got out of the tub. I put on my Christmas lingerie and walked out of the bathroom. Darryl was laying on the bed, watching television. He must have been deep into it because he didn't even hear me come out. I cleared my throat, and he turned around.

"Well, what do we have here? My very own Christmas

gift. Merry Christmas to me!"

He turned off the television and cut some music on.

"Now come over here and let me unwrap my gift."

I started walking over towards him.

"Walk slow. We got all night baby. While you are at it. Do that lil dance for me."

I walked to the middle of the floor and danced for Darryl. It's something Darryl loves for me to do when I dress up in lingerie for him. As many of strip clubs I had to pull Calvin out of; I've learned a few tricks or so over the years. Darryl approached me, but I pushed him back on the bed.

It was written all over his face that he loved how I dominated and commanded the room. And I loved the attention he gave me when he saw me dance. I loved the feeling it gave me. Power and desire. It was a high I didn't want to come down from. I danced some more for him. I started walking towards Darryl and stood in front of him. I unhooked one part of my bra to make it easier for him.

"Unwrap your gift. This toy is ready to be played with."

Darryl spun me around and held me from behind by my hips. He started to kiss me down my back. He ignited a fire in me! He unzipped and unhooked the rest of my lingerie. He spun me around again and cupped my breast. He was so gentle and so passionate with me. He reached up to my shoulders and slid the lingerie off of me. I pushed him down on the bed. I climbed on top of him until I reached his face. I positioned myself and felt his tongue doing a dance under me. I felt his tongue tasting me as if he was famished. He then held on to my ass and I grinded his face. Hard. I found my rhythm and stayed there until I was reaching climax.

"I'm. About. To. Cum."

I held onto the headboard as I released. I then laid down on all fours and let Darryl enter me from the back.

This was a moment I didn't want to end.

Christmas Day

We woke up the next morning and had breakfast in bed. At about 11AM, we began loading the gifts into the car and headed over to my parents' house. We arrived and found a spot to park close to the driveway. I saw so many people in the neighborhood that I haven't seen since Christmas of 2016. I waved and said hello to them all. It was so good to see everyone. It felt good to be home.

I grabbed Darryl's hand and squeezed it.

"You ready to meet the fam?"

"I sure am. Let's do this."

We walked in and my parents were waiting at the door.

"Mom, Dad. Could y'all be less weird?"

They laughed.

"We just wanted to meet the man that is taking care of

our baby out there in Texas."

My daddy then called out to some of my cousins to take the gifts and put them under the tree.

"Merry Christmas, Mr. and Mrs. Stevenson. My name is Darryl Glover."

Darryl extended his hand to my parents and they shook hands.

"And I'm Tracy Stevenson." Tracy said as she slid in from the kitchen.

"Hi, Tracy. I have heard so much about you. It's nice to finally meet you."

"Yea, I'm sure my sister said some wild things. Don't believe her."

Darryl laughed.

"I told her I would see for myself."

"Darryl let's get you away from these women and go watch some football. Alabama got a game on right now. These women have some more food to cook, let's leave them to it!"

My dad joked as he and Darryl walked off into the living room.

My mom, Tracy and I went into the kitchen. My mom opened the oven and I saw her golden, buttery cornbread being pulled out. She sat it on top of the stove, next to the greens. My mouth instantly began to water. We prepared plates for my dad, Darryl, and a few elder family members. We then brought the food out and let everyone else makes their own plates. We came back into the kitchen, poured a glass of wine, and ate our food at the island. Our Christmas tradition.

"So, tell me what do y'all think of Darryl so far?"

"Any man that has the idea of bringing my daughters back together is alright in my book. I'm glad he came into your life and knocked some sense into you."

"Wow Mama! Tell me how you really feel." I said as my mom laughed.

Tracy then chimed in.

"Well, you already know how I feel. Any man is better than that piece of trash, Calvin. I'm happy to see you smile again. *Genuinely* smile. I know when you're happy and when you're not. And I can tell you are happy. And that makes me happy."

"Well, I'm glad to hear you guys think highly of him. He does make me happy. My mind is clear, and I don't have to worry about him hurting me emotionally. I feel free."

"That's alright, baby. I'm happy to hear that." My mom said as she squeezed my hand.

We finished our food and went into the living room. Everyone was either talking, watching television, on their phones, or still eating. I took a moment to take it all in. I missed my family and spending quality time with them. I snuggled up on the couch, sitting in between my Dad and Darryl.

"So, what have y'all two been talking about out here?"

"You and football. This man told me he had to jump through hoops just to get you. I told him that's because I raised you right." My daddy said with a smile.

"Yes, you did Daddy." I looked over at Darryl and winked.

We continued watching the game. I enjoyed watching my daddy and Darryl cheer at the game together. I was so happy that Darryl was blending in so well with my family. It felt so natural. I later got up and went to the bathroom. I came out and my dad was standing outside the door.

"Come in here." He was motioning for me to walk into their bedroom.

I went into the room and sat at my mom's vanity. He sat on the bed.

"You know I stay out of your business and try not to get too involved. I just want to know that you know what you're doing. I would hate to be all the way here in Montgomery, while you're in Texas with an angry Calvin. I don't want him getting jealous or upset that you're seeing someone else and take it out on you. Especially since divorce paperwork hasn't been drawn up. I know he's divorcing you, but I'm a man. And I know that us men can be very territorial. Are you sure you and Calvin are over?"

"Yes, daddy. I'm sure. We haven't talked in over a year.

I'm not sure why he hasn't presented any divorce papers. I'll let him handle that though. I have too much on my plate now to be worried about it."

"Just be sure, honey. I can't protect you in Houston."

"I understand, daddy. And I appreciate your concern. But I don't want to keep talking about Calvin. What do you think about Darryl? I need to know."

"He's a good man, baby girl. We talked about his family and upbringing, his job, and a few other things I'll keep to myself. I can tell he's ready to complete his life and settle down with a good woman."

"Oh, I'm so glad to hear you say that daddy. You know I value your opinion."

"Of course. You know I'm a man of few words. And if I see anything wrong, I'll let you know. But I can't say too many bad things about him. Unlike that bastard you married."

"Alright, alright Daddy. I already know how you feel about Calvin. Let's get back to the game."

We walked out of the room and I went back into the living room where everyone else was. My dad went in the kitchen by my mother. I sat back in the same spot next to Darryl and leaned over to him.

"My daddy likes you." I whispered and said with a smile.

"I'm D. Glove baby. I charm the ladies and the daddies." He said with a smile.

"Whatever. Stop charming my daddy, punk." I joked.

I sat back up and finished watching television. Shortly after, Tracy came in with a deck of cards.

"Who's ready to get their ass whipped in Spades?"

I looked at Darryl.

"You know how to play?"

"Girl, please. Do you know who you talking to? Let's whip some ass!"

I laughed out loud.

"Me and Darryl are ready. Let's go, Tracy!"

After much eating, opening presents, watching football, and playing cards; Darryl and I were getting ready to head out for the night. I hugged and kissed my family goodbye. I hugged Tracy a bit longer. It felt good to have my sister back. We promised to stay in touch with each other more. And she promised that she would come and visit me; and I could show her a good time in Houston.

It also felt good that Darryl had met my family and they liked him. I was really happy that Daddy liked him. He was never too fond of Calvin; so, this put my mind at ease. I had their blessing and finally felt like I could move on with my life.

We arrived back at the hotel and began packing. We were heading out on a flight tomorrow afternoon because we both had to get back to work. After packing, Darryl drew us a bubble bath. He poured us a glass of wine, and we relaxed in the tub.

"I've really enjoyed my time on this trip with you. Thank you for doing this for me. You have really helped in bringing my sister and I back together. Just spending time with my family and you all together meant the world to me. Words can't express how much I appreciate it."

"Sure baby. I could not imagine me and Daniel beefing for any reason, especially over a woman. Every group or pair of siblings need that bond. I am happy that I could help. Now be quiet before you kill my buzz, woman." Darryl joked.

I laid in his arms and relaxed. It wasn't long before I felt his hands rubbing all over me, caressing my naked body. I then felt him growing under me.

"I guess I didn't kill your buzz after all."

"Nope, it's just getting started."

After making love in the tub, Darryl and I got out and went straight to sleep. Hours later, I was awakened by my phone going off. I silenced it, but it kept vibrating back-to-back. I started to think it was my family, and I wondered if something was wrong. I looked at my phone, and I had five missed calls.

To my surprise, they were all from Calvin. What the hell did he want? I looked back at Darryl, and he was still sleeping peacefully. My phone started ringing again. It was Calvin. I went into the bathroom and answered the phone.

"Calvin? Is something wrong? What do you want?"

Chapter 14

Darryl-Houston, TX

Valentine's Day 2019

"This girl got you over there cooking! What's in them pots and pans bro?"

"Blackened salmon, potatoes au gratin, and broccolini. Oh, yea. She's going to fall in love tonight." I joked with Daniel.

"Well, I'll let you go. I do not want you messing up the dinner and blaming it on me. I'm on the way to dinner with Jalisa. Talk to you later baby boy, love ya."

"Love you too." I heard Jalisa say over the phone.

"I love y'all too. Bye." I hung up the phone and tended to my potatoes in the oven.

It had been two months since our trip to Alabama. It was nice to see Tiffany and her sister back on speaking terms, and the happiness those conversations brought her.

I checked the time, and she was a little later than usual. I called and checked on her. No answer. I didn't realize it was thirty minutes past the time she was supposed to be here. And she's never late. She finally arrived and knocked on the door. I opened the door, and she had a sad look on her face.

"Tiffany baby, are you okay? You don't look so good."

"Darryl, we need to talk."

Tiffany slowly walked into the house.

"What's up Tiff? I was starting to worry about you."

Tiffany stood with her back turned to me. I walked up to her and tried to remove her coat from her. But she didn't budge. Her body language was stiff.

"Darryl, I don't know how to say this to you."

I backed up, embracing myself for what she was about to say.

"Whatever it is Tiffany, just say it."

She remained standing with her back turned to me. She took a deep sigh, and then spoke with trembles in her voice.

"Calvin reached out to me. We have been talking for the past two months and are going to try to work things out. We're getting back together, and I have to cut things off between you and I."

I had to process what she was saying.

"Say what now, Tiffany?"

I heard her sniffling.

"Tiffany, what did you say?"

I heard Tiffany struggling to speak through her tears.

"I'm so sorry, Darryl."

"You're kidding me, right? You're really going back to your husband?"

"Darryl, I told you this could happen. It was always on the table."

"Tiffany don't do this. Don't do this to us. Don't do this to yourself. Let's talk about this. Please."

"Darryl, he just came to me out of the blue. I wasn't expecting it at all."

I stood there speechless.

"Say something Darryl. Please don't make this hard for me."

Don't make it hard for her? How dare she only be concerned about herself when she was breaking up with me? I lost it and anger came over me.

"What the fuck, Tiffany! Hard for you? You let this motherfucker back in? After all this time? After all the shit he has done! Dragged you across the country just to leave you high and dry? Assed out? Separated and sabotaged your relationship with your family? The family I helped you mend back together!"

Tiffany turned around and looked at me.

"I'm sorry, Darryl." She walked over to me and lifted her arms in attempt to hug me.

"I can't fucking believe you, Tiffany! Don't touch me!" I jerked my arm away from her.

"I told you from the beginning Darryl I still wanted to be with him. I told you I was willing to work things out with him if the chance ever presented itself. I told you no strings attached. And you agreed, Darryl. You agreed! You said you can walk away when the time came."

"Fuck that, Tiffany! I said if the time came. *IF!* I never thought it would. How was I not supposed to catch feelings for you, when you knew I already had them? You knew how I felt about you. Damn Tiffany! I thought you was stronger than this, better than this, smarter than this!"

Tiffany stood there with tears streaming down her face.

"Darryl, I'm sorry. I can't help that I still love him. He is my husband. I—"

I cut her off.

"Save it Tiffany. I am not about to sit here and listen to you profess your love for another man. You had something real with me. You had someone who would have given you the world. Yet, you still choose to run behind the man who fucked over you more than once. The man who made you look like a goddamn fool. Get the fuck out!"

Tiffany gasped.

"Darryl, really?"

Tiffany came up and tried to hug me again.

"Can we at least still be friends? We still have to work together, and I don't want this to be awkward."

I took her arms from around me.

"I don't want to be *just* your friend, Tiffany. We're way beyond that. Leave my house please."

"Darryl, please. We were friends before any of this happened, and I just want things to go back to the way we were. I don't want to lose that. I don't want to lose you."

I walked to my door and opened it.

"Leave Tiffany. I'm not going to say it again."

Tiffany walked past me and stepped outside. She turned around, about to say something.

"I don't want to hear it, Tiffany! Leave before I say something I'll regret!"

She turned around and walked to her car. I slammed the door. I heard her car turn on and drive off. I sat down on my recliner and rubbed my temples. This hurt. The thought of losing her hurts. The thought of her going back to her husband hurts. *God, it hurts!* This was a pain I never felt before.

Shortly after, I received a text. It was Tiffany.

"I took a week off vacation to give you some space. Hopefully you'll find it in your heart to forgive me and we can be friends again. I'm sorry."

The oven timer went off and broke my concentration. The food was ready. The Valentine's Day dinner I prepared for us was ready.

I angrily tossed my phone to the other side of the house and heard it break apart.

"Fucking bitch!" I shouted out.

My night was officially ruined.

The Next Morning

I woke up to breakfast in the air. The holy trinity was at it again. Grits, bacon and eggs. I looked around and saw my pants and boxers on the floor. I put them on and headed downstairs. Carmen was pouring a glass of orange juice and turned around.

"Hey sleepy head. Thought I was going to have to come up there and get you, but I see my cooking beat me to it."

Carmen sat my plate and juice down on the island.

"How you feeling baby? Talk to Mama."

I took a couple bites of my breakfast.

"I'm just so disappointed, Carmen. This clown just creeps back in after all this time. And she just let him back in. It's like, how dumb can she be?"

"She's not dumb, Darryl. She is confused, hurt, and technically, she's still married. That is a chance you took deciding to mess with her. And you can't blame her. She told you what it was in the beginning. That it was a possibility. You can't be mad that it actually came to pass."

"Whose side are you on here, Carmen?"

"I just want you to realize what's happening here. It's karma Darryl, sorry to tell you. Think about all them women you have dated who thought they had a chance with you. And when you dogged them, you couldn't care less. Because you told them what it was from the beginning."

"What we had was special. It was different than what I was doing with these other women before her."

"Special or not. Fact remains the same. She told you what it was from the beginning."

"I just can't believe it went down like that."

"I hear you baby. I'm pretty sure she's not done with you, though. Just give her time, she'll be back."

"Nah, forget her. I'm not taking her back after she played me."

"Yea, yea whatever. Finish your breakfast so you can get out of here and pick up your new phone. Can't believe you threw a temper tantrum and broke your damn phone. And don't forget to leave the key for me. I'll be over there later."

I finished up my breakfast and left Carmen's home. I went over to the AT&T store and purchased the latest iPhone. I needed an upgrade anyway. After the worker helped me transfer everything over, my phone started buzzing nonstop. I walked out of the store, watching the notifications build up. Work emails, social media posts, and more. Then, texts started pouring in. I scrolled over them until I saw Tiffany's messages.

I clicked on her name.

9:42PM: "I'm sorry, Darryl. I tried calling you. Did you block me? It keeps going straight to voicemail."

10:25PM: "I still want to be friends. I value our friendship more than anything."

10:53PM: "Talk to me, Darryl. Please."

11:17PM: "Please stop ignoring me."

11:54PM: "Ok, I'll give you your space. Call me when you're ready."

I wanted to reply so bad. I clicked on the respond box, then closed the message app out. I did that back and forth for some time. So many feelings and emotions I had. So much anger I felt. Yet I still wanted to be with her. I decided against texting her back. The only thing I wanted to hear her say, was that she made a mistake and wanted to get back with me. But if she wasn't going to say that; I didn't want to hear it.

So many questions started running through my head. How often were they talking? Was she talking to him when she was coming over to my house? Or when I was at her place? How long was she contemplating on going back to him? What did he say that won her over? How convincing was he? Did they sleep together? Did he make her cum like I did?

Man, I feel played! She played with my feelings after everything I have done to make her forget her husband. Only to go back to him. Forget it and forget her!

I drove home and chilled out until it was time to meet Daniel. I was meeting him for a drink at The Davenport. Needed some brotherly advice and a good drink. He expected that I would be doing some heavy drinking, so he decided to pick me up.

Shortly after, I received a call from Daniel telling me that he was outside. I locked up, left the key under the mat for Carmen, and headed to his car.

"What's up bro? How ya feeling?" Daniel asked as soon as I got into the car.

"I'm doing good. Ready to hit this spot and get my drink on."

The rest of the car ride was silent. We arrived at the spot, sat at the bar, and ordered our drinks. The Godfather was my favorite and what I was in the mood for tonight.

"Alright man, tell me what's going on."

"I lost her, man. Lost her to her husband. How ironic is that? What was I thinking? You were right." I sipped on my drink.

"You were thinking with your heart and not your head. Don't beat yourself up. You can't control who you love. Besides that puppy love shit, this was the first woman you really loved. I know it's hard for you. It shocked us all that you were finally settling down."

"That's what bothers me the most. I really had feelings for her. Carmen said its karma. For all the hearts I've broken."

"Carmen? You are seeing her again? Already?"

"Yea, I saw her last night. I was so mad, I needed to release my frustrations. She's actually going to be at my house later."

"You sure don't skip a beat. How you going to be crying over one woman, but sleeping with another one? Give yourself some time, bro. Process this before you run to another woman."

"Hey, Tiffany broke things off with me. What was I supposed to do?"

"I guess. Anyway, back to the situation at hand. Tiffany will be back around. You made that woman happy after years of being heartbroken and humiliated. Trust me, she's going to come back."

I shrugged my shoulders. My phone started buzzing. I checked it. Tiffany was calling. I considered answering but didn't. I silenced my phone and ordered another drink. It was well needed.

After getting our drink on and much needed conversation, me and Daniel were riding out Westheimer on the way home. Daniel pulled out a blunt and handed it to me. I fired it up and took a hit. I missed the days of us cruising, drinking and smoking. With the windows rolled down, catching the breeze.

"Puff, puff, pass my brother. Stop hogging the joint." Daniel said with his hand out ready for me to pass the blunt.

I handed it to him and zoned out to the music. We arrived at my home and he parked in the driveway. I got out the car and walked over to his side.

"Alright big bro. Thanks for the advice and free liquor." I joked.

I heard my door open and I turned around. Carmen walked over to us and kissed me.

"I see you've been drinking all evening, huh? I taste it all on your lips."

"Yea, I had a few."

"Well, I have another glass poured for you too when you get inside."

She then turned to Daniel.

"Hey there stranger! Long time no see." She smiled at him.

"Hey there, Carmen! It's good to see you." He then looked up at me and smugly smirked.

Suddenly, we heard a car turn on and speed off down the street. Their brakes screeched loud when they got to the stop sign. Then they sped off out of the neighborhood. It looked like Tiffany's car, but it was going so fast; I couldn't call it. Me and Daniel looked at each other and shrugged our shoulders.

Probably was a drunk driver.

Daniel reached out the window and waved to Carmen.

"Alright Carmen. Goodnight, honey."

"Hit me when you get home and let me know you made it safely. Seems to be some crazy people out here on the road tonight. Love you."

"Love you too."

Daniel pulled off and I watched him get to the street sign. I went inside and sat on my recliner, watching television until I finished my glass of Hennessey. Twenty minutes later I got a text from Daniel.

"Made it inside."

I sent him a thumbs up emoji. I then showered and joined Carmen in the bed.

I arrived at work Monday evening, and it felt a bit awkward knowing I was going to be faced with Tiffany. I got settled in and waited for her to arrive. But instead of Tiffany walking in, Jimmy did. Jimmy was the morning engineer.

"Hey what's up, D.? I'm not sure if Tiffany told you, but she's on vacation. I'll be filling in for her this week."

I had to think about it. She did tell me she was going on vacation.

"Yea, she told me. Look forward to working with you,

brother."

I lied. I wanted to see Tiffany.

Jimmy did a head nod and headed into the engineer's room. Once he was all settled in, we got all tuned up and ready to go.

"Alright, alright. It's Midnight Love, with ya boy D. Glove. Turning up this Houston heat, while you lay in your sheets. Giving you tunes so smooth, aiming to put you in the groove. I want to talk to the fellas tonight. Men, have you ever been heartbroken? Call in with your stories and talk to ya boy."

The week passed by and things weren't the same without Tiffany. No more walks to the car, laughing and talking along the way. She finally was here long enough to get a permanent spot on the first floor. But I still enjoyed walking her to her car and making sure she got out of the parking lot safely. It was weird without our nightly routine. I wondered how the vibe would be when she came back to work Monday.

Over the weekend I hooked up with Daniel and Jalisa.

When I got to their house, Jalisa greeted me with a smile and hug. We walked into the kitchen and sat at the island.

"How are you feeling, Darryl? I heard what happened and I just want to say I feel for you. I know how much you liked Tiffany. Hell, I really liked her too. Have you talked to her at all?"

"Nah. I gave her some space. Have you talked to her?"

"I didn't know if she felt comfortable talking to me about it. And I didn't know how you would feel if I reached out to her. So, I just left it alone."

I shrugged my shoulders.

"For what it's worth. I don't think things will work out between her and her husband. She really had feelings for you. And she really appreciated how you helped her with her family. That is all she ever talked about since Christmas. She may be confused at the moment. But she really cares about you. Just give her some time and space to figure herself out."

"Thank you, Jalisa. But I don't see that happening. I doubt if I even want her back. She played me; I don't know if I can come back from that."

"You can play that macho role with your brother. But it's not working on me. I know how much you liked her. If she wanted you back, you'd take her back."

I put my head down. She saw straight through me.

Jalisa continued.

"I know your ego is bruised; but don't give up. I have never seen you head over heels for a woman like this in all the 14 years I've known you. I've watched women walk in and out of your life. You've never treated any of them the way you treated Tiffany."

Jalisa lifted my head so she could look me in the eyes.

"And now I hear you are back to seeing Carmen. You know I'm not too fond of her, but that's your decision. Just don't give up so easily on Tiffany. She's the one. Do you hear me?"

I nodded my head yes.

"Thanks, sis."

"You're welcome, lil bro. Look, I know you're hurting. But it'll get better."

She gave me another hug and kissed me on the forehead. Daniel finally came with the keys, and we headed out to poetry night. The third wheel trio was back at it again.

The weekend seemed to come and go quickly. That damn Monday came back faster than ever.

I anticipated seeing Tiffany at work tonight. After thinking it over, I wanted to apologize for how I talked to her. We were friends before we hooked up, and I was willing to put my pride aside and become her friend again. I must admit that I did enjoy our friendship and companionship. I also missed it.

I arrived at work, ready to face Tiffany. I walked in and saw Jimmy in the engineer booth again. Why was he in the booth? I tried to think of a way to approach him without asking why was still here. And where the hell was Tiffany?

"Hey there Jimmy. Tiffany still on vacation?" That was the best line I could think of.

"Nah man, funny thing happened. We were able to swap shifts. Remember when I was telling you how crazy it has been trying to maintain my work schedule with my new Spring Semester schedule? Well, I mentioned it to Tiffany after working the night shift last week. Out of the blue, she offered to swap with me. And we got it cleared with HR this morning. What a blessing, right? Looks like you got to get used to me from now on." Jimmy joked.

I fake laughed.

"Nah man that's great! I'm glad it all worked out for you. Look at God, right?"

I was not happy about this.

"Thanks, man. Give me a few minutes and we can start the show."

What the hell! How dare she jump shifts like that? I couldn't believe the extremities she was going to just to avoid me! I bet that husband of hers had something to do with it. Or she felt guilty about continuing to work with me. I walked out of the station and called her. She didn't answer. I called again. She sent me to voicemail. So, I sent a text message.

"It's like that? You just jump shifts on me and don't even say anything? That's wrong, Tiffany. I thought we were better than that. And you wanted to be 'friends', right?"

Instantly, I saw the three bubbles pop up. She must've been waiting on me to text her. She knew what she was doing. The bubbles disappeared. They came back and disappeared again. Then she finally sent her message through.

"Fuck you, Darryl. Leave me alone. Do you."

Fuck me? Do me? What did that mean? Where was this attitude coming from? She left me, and then have the nerve to catch an attitude? I called her again and was sent to voicemail after a few rings. I called again, and it went straight to voicemail. She must have blocked me. Okay, I see how it is.

Chapter 15

Tiffany

March 2019

I sat on the bed, pondering over my decisions. A month had passed by, and I couldn't stop thinking about how things went down with Darryl and me. I missed him terribly. It had been a long four weeks without him.

Calvin was trying to do things right this time. But this wasn't anything new. Every time he cheated and came back; he played the good boy role until he messed up and cheated again. The flowers, candy, cards, dinners, gifts; he rolled out all the tricks. But I was getting tired of this dance and tango that we were doing. I questioned if I should've just let it go. But I didn't want to give up on my marriage. I said I would fight for my marriage, for better or for worse. I gave God my word on that. But sometimes I wonder if God is trying to tell me something. Did I make the right decision? Should I have chosen Darryl?

Should I have chosen my happiness?

So many thoughts were running through my mind.

I looked around the room, and it just didn't feel right being here. At Calvin's place. Calvin had moved out of the house we first lived in, into a new one. He tried over and over to get me to call it our home, but this wasn't my home. My home was still at my apartment. I still had it because I was not ready to fully move back in with Calvin yet. I wanted to take things slow this time. I wanted to give this situation my undivided attention. I'd rather be safe than sorry.

I glanced over at Calvin, and he was knocked out sleep in the bed. Snoring loud enough to wake the neighbors. I looked up at the television and Martin was on BET. Something Darryl and I always watched to pass time. I thought about the laughs we shared while watching our favorite show. My mind then wandered about what he was doing at the moment.

I often wondered if Darryl was thinking about me as well. If he still cared about me. Because I damn sure still cared about him. My thoughts shifted to the way he made me feel. How appreciated he made me feel. How caring he was towards me. How he made me feel beautiful. How passionate he was. How hot he made me. How he made me release every time we made love!

I looked over at Calvin again. His face was doing that twitching thing he does when he's getting deeper into his slumber. Ugh! I hated it. Disgust came over me. I started to think about how Calvin never made me feel the way Darryl made me feel. Over the years of Calvin and I being together, I've never came as many times with him as I had with Darryl. Not only did Darryl stimulate me mentally and emotionally; I couldn't deny the stimulation he gave me sexually.

The more I thought about Darryl, I couldn't take it anymore. I grabbed my phone, went into the bathroom and turned on the faucet. I sat on the toilet and called him. I knew he probably just made it home from work and was still up.

The last time we talked, I cursed him out; after seeing him with that older woman. I was nervous to see how he was going to respond to me. But in this moment, I really didn't care. I needed to see him. The phone rang three times before he answered.

"Tiffany, what do you want? It's 1AM. Why are you calling me?"

I froze for a moment. Hearing his voice made me feel some type of way. Even if he was mad at me.

"Tiffany! What do you want?" He screamed into the phone.

"Can I come over?" Was all I managed to get out.

"For what?"

"To talk. I really need to talk to you."

"You can talk over the phone, Tiffany."

"I want to see you. I need to see you." I said in a moment of weakness.

My body was yearning for him by this time.

"Oh, now you want to talk? It doesn't work like that. I've been calling you and texting you for the last month. No response. And suddenly you call me out of the blue with some 'you want to talk' shit? Talk to your husband. Because I'm—"

I cut him off mid-sentence.

"I miss you, Darryl. God, I miss you so much. Can I come over? I need you baby. Please."

I heard him take a deep breath in and sigh.

"Okay, Tiffany. Come on." He then hung up the phone.

I jumped up from the toilet and snatched off my bonnet. I brushed my teeth and washed myself at the sink. I quietly went back into the bedroom and put on some sexy lingerie for Darryl. I threw on a black bodycon dress and grabbed a pair of sandals. I looked back at Calvin, and he was still in a deep sleep. I tiptoed out of the bedroom, grabbed my purse and keys, and damn near ran out of the house. I got in the car and made a straight shot to Darryl's.

When I pulled into Darryl's driveway, a sense of nervousness came over me. I missed him so much though, I couldn't let nerves get in the way. I walked up to the door and knocked on it. Darryl slightly opened the door and just stared at me.

"Well, are you going to let me in?"

"I'm not sure if I should. You did some foul shit. And you think you can just come over here when you want?"

"If you didn't want me here, you wouldn't have told me to come over. Do you want me to leave? I will if you want me to."

Darryl walked off and left the door open. I walked in and closed the door behind me. Darryl stood with his back turned to me at the kitchen counter.

"Why, Tiffany? Why did you take him back? Why did you leave me for him?"

"He's my husband, Darryl. I was honest with you from the beginning. I told you if he wanted to work it out, I would give it another try. I never lied to you about that."

"I don't understand you. You had somebody who would give you the world. And yet you chose to go back to that piece of shit! I just don't get it."

I instantly got defensive. I deflected from myself and threw things back on him out of being nervous. It was the only card I had left to throw down.

"Don't act like you're a saint. I saw you with that woman the day after I left. You got some nerve. You were probably with her the whole time you were with me."

Darryl finally turned around and faced me. I stayed my distance at the door.

"What woman?"

"The older woman I saw come out of your house. When you were in the driveway talking to Daniel. I saw y'all kissing."

"What, are you stalking me now?"

"No, I had been trying to get in touch with you all day. But you weren't answering the phone. I came here and waited for you. And when you came home, you were with her. It reminded me of seeing Calvin with that woman. I sped off and said forget it."

"So that *was* you who pulled off real fast, speeding down the street? I thought I recognized your car."

"Yep. I came back here to make it right. I was going to leave my husband for you. That's what I came back here to tell you. But you obviously didn't care enough anyway. And that's why I changed my work shift. I didn't want to see you anymore. So, I wrote you off."

"Oh, and I guess that's why you cursed me out and told me to do me?"

"Yep. I am done with you men hurting me!"

"*I* never hurt you. Don't guilt trip me and make it seem like *I* ruined what could've been. *You left me, remember?* Whatever I chose to do with whomever, is my business. Don't you dare flip it and put the blame on me. And if you're so done, why are you here?"

"Who is she?"

"An old friend."

"Who is she?"

"An old friend."

"An old friend?"

"Yep."

I paused to think about what I was doing. I had no business being mad at him and getting defensive. He was right; he was able to do whatever he wanted to do. And besides, I didn't come over here to fuss. I came here to be with Darryl, and I wasn't about to let some old broad ruin that for me. Enough of the talking.

I took off my sandals and slid out of my dress. I stood there, wearing my best lingerie. Knowing I looked damn good, and better than that older woman he's screwing.

"You miss me?" I asked him as I walked over to him.

We started kissing. No matter how angry he was with me; he couldn't deny he still wanted me. Darryl gripped my ass and caressed the rest of my body. I felt him growing underneath me. I dropped down to my knees and released him from his boxers. I covered him with my mouth.

"Ooh shit, baby." Was all he could manage to say.

He grabbed the back of my head with one hand. I got my rhythm going and devoured him. I could feel him getting weak in the knees and heard him whispering out soft moans. I looked up at him and he was staring dead at me. It's like he was looking into my soul. It wasn't long before I saw his eyes roll back and then he closed his eyes. I knew what that meant, and I wasn't ready for him to release just yet. I got up, walking him into the living room. I sat him down on the couch and got on top of him. He slid my panties to the side, and I eased onto him. I took a ride. *A wild, long ride.*

We both came at the same time. It was euphoric! I collapsed down on him; both of us breathing out of control. I tried getting up, but he held onto me. He didn't want to let me go. I held onto him back. I didn't want to let him go either. I missed being in his arms. I missed smelling his scent. I missed his companionship. I missed us.

My mind drifted to thinking about the choices I've made. I hated that I didn't have the answers. All I did know was that this moment felt right. Even if it was only for right now.

We ended Round 2 in the shower, cleaning ourselves off from Round 1. I couldn't get enough of this man! We went into the bedroom and fell asleep.

I woke up at 5:00AM to my phone buzzing non-stop. It buzzed so much that it fell off the nightstand, on to the floor. 10 Messages, 12 Missed Calls, and 5 Voicemails. All from Calvin. Reality hit me and snatched me from my fairytale. I still had a husband at home.

I peeled Darryl's arm from around me, creeped into the bathroom; and called Calvin. He greeted me yelling.

"Tiffany, where are you?! I've been calling you for two hours!"

I tried to sound as sleepy as I could. I also tried to lie as best as I could.

"Oh my goodness, Cal. I lost track of time. Lauren got stranded and needed someone to help her get home. After we made it to her house, I was so tired. I passed out on her couch."

"Why didn't you wake me up and tell me you were leaving?"

"You were sleeping so peacefully; I didn't want to wake you. I'm so sorry."

"Just get back home, okay? Do you want me to come meet you over there and follow you back home? I don't want you on the road this time of hour by yourself."

"No!" I said urgently. "I'll leave right now. Be home soon!"

I quickly hung up the phone.

I stepped back into the bedroom, and Darryl was still sleeping in the bed. I quietly gathered my clothes and began putting them back on. I grabbed my purse and was about to head out the door.

"So, it's like that? You were going to leave without saying goodbye? He calls and you go running again."

Shit, I thought he was asleep! I turned around and he was sitting up on the bed, watching my every move.

"I'm sorry, Darryl."

"You know, Tiffany. I'm getting really tired of hearing you say you're sorry. I'm not someone that's going to be your go to guy. You can't just dump me and pick me up when you want to. I'm not a toy. I have feelings. I thought you came back here to be with me. Not to use me. Get out, Tiffany! Lose my number!"

"Darryl! Please don't act like that. I don't want to lose you. I love you!"

"You don't love me. You're too confused to love me. You only love yourself."

I tried walking over to Darryl and hugging him, but he wasn't having it.

"What do you want from me, Tiffany? Huh? You want me to sit around, waiting for you to come back? You want to be with your husband all day, and squeeze in a couple hours with me when you can? Or let me guess. You want him Monday through Friday; and I get you on the weekends? That ain't happening!"

"I want to be with you. I really do. I—"

Darryl cut me off mid-sentence.

"You want to have your cake and eat it too. That's what you want. You know, you told me you were messed up and had issues from the beginning. I should've believed you. Get out Tiffany. I don't have time for this shit!"

I didn't know what to say. I didn't want to leave. I wanted to stay. I wanted to leave Calvin for Darryl; but things were so complicated.

"If you really want me to, I'll leave you alone for good." I said, holding out for an ounce of hope.

"I want you to leave me alone for good. Bye, Tiffany." He said with no hesitation.

I grabbed the rest of my things and left the room.

"Shut the door behind you." Darryl called out.

I shut the door behind me, got into my car, and drove off.

I parked around the corner and cried my heart out. I cried for the pain I caused Darryl. For the stupidity I felt for going back to Calvin. For the devoted woman inside of me who was confused and hurting. All she wanted was to be genuinely loved, and I kept her deprived from it.

I wiped my tears and headed home. I had to go face the man I had learned to resent. The man I called my husband. Calvin Goddamn Willow.

Chapter 16

Darryl

March 2019

I pulled up at Daniel's house, and met him and Jalisa out back on their patio. I gave Daniel a fist bump and Jalisa a hug. Jalisa sat down a pitcher of Bud Lights. She went into the kitchen, came back out with bags of crawfish, and placed it on the table. She sat down with us, rolled up a joint, and fired up. She took a few puffs, and then let Daniel take a few puffs before taking it back. She left us to talk. We opened the bags and got to work.

"So, what's been up these past two weeks man? You still haven't heard from Tiffany after she left out again?" Daniel said as he peeled crawfish.

"Nah, I haven't heard from her. She called me a few times, but I never answered. I don't feel like hearing her apologize again. It's only going to make me more frustrated."

"I'm sorry this happened to you, D. I know how much you were feeling her."

"Can I just enjoy this crawfish and beer with my brother? No Tiffany talk."

"Aright, man. You got it."

Daniel and I smoke, drank and talked for the next hour. We then went inside to watch a game. A few hours later, I was on my way out the door. Jalisa came walking out and stopped me at the car.

"I will let you go after I say this one thing. I know you still love Tiffany, and I know she still loves you."

"I don't want to hear that, Jalisa. She made her choice. She—"

"Just listen to me. I wanted to let you know that she called me the day after she left your house that night. She's really shook up about this."

"Jalisa, why are you still in contact with her? When she left me this time, I expected everyone to understand that she also left this family. You're outta line for that."

"She became my friend too, Darryl. What was I supposed to do?"

I shook my head at Jalisa.

"Anyway, she called me that next day. Crying. Unsure of what she should do. She is stuck between a rock and a hard place."

"I don't see what's so hard about it. I know I treat her better than her husband ever did."

"You're not married Darryl, and you will never understand until you are. Marriages can be complicated. Marriage is not something people are so freely to give up. You make a promise to God that you would stick it out through thick and thin. Well, right now she feels like this is her thick and thin. And she's questioning herself on what she should do. Give her some space and time to heal."

"I don't have that kind of time to wait around for her to get her shit together."

"You can play like you don't have time. But you do. You still love her. Just give her some time. She'll be back."

"She made her choice when she used me then went back to her husband."

"Now, I'm not going to deny that her having sex with you and leaving you wasn't foul. She was wrong for playing with your emotions like that. But ain't no woman going to leave her home, with her husband sleeping in the bed; to come see a man that she doesn't love. That's a big risk, and she took it for you. She still loves you, and she still wants to be with you. Trust your big sister on this please. Now give me a hug and get outta here."

I gave Jalisa a hug, got in my car and drove off. I thought about going to Carmen's home to pass some time, but I didn't want to. So, I decided to go home.

I got inside the house and stretched out on the couch. I turned on the television and watched old reruns of Martin. It wasn't long until I drifted off to sleep.

A few hours later, I was awakened by banging on the door. I thought I was tripping, but the banging continued. As I got closer to the door, I heard a man and a woman yelling.

"Open this door, motherfucker! I know you're in there!"

I didn't recognize the man's voice, but I did recognize Tiffany's voice.

"Calvin, you are not about to do this. Let's go!"

But Calvin continued banging on my door. And Tiffany kept yelling at him to stop.

Now was the time. I always wanted to meet Calvin. I've always wondered who the man was who hurt Tiffany. I've always wondered who the man was married to my woman.

I went into my bedroom, searching for my pistol. I wasn't going to meet this man with my fists alone. I damn sure could take him. But as angry as he sounds, I didn't know what he had for me. I made it back to the door and opened it. Expecting the worst.

"Man, I'm going to tell you one time and one time only. Get your ass off my doorstep!"

"I'm not going anywhere until I beat your ass."

"I'm telling you. This ain't what you want, Calvin."

"I said, I'm not going anywhere until I beat your ass. Keep your hands off my fucking wife!"

"Just my hands? Or my dick too?"

Calvin then took a swing at me. Knocked me right in the jaw. I thought about shooting him, but I haven't kicked someone's ass in a while. I put my gun down.

"Oh, you had a gun? Can't fight with your fists like a man?"

Calvin then swung at me again, but I blocked it. I quickly swung back at him. We started going at it and fell to the ground. He got a few licks on me, but I was getting the best of him. All I could hear was Tiffany shouting as my fists pounded his now bloody face.

"Oh my god! Stop you two! Darryl, you're going to kill him! Stop!!!!"

Hearing her piercing scream broke me out of my rage. I got off him and stepped back onto my doorstep. Tiffany helped him back up on his feet.

"I told you this ain't what you want. Take your ass home before I actually use my gun and send you home for real." I warned him while breathing hard, in a rage.

Tiffany helped Calvin back to the car and helped him in.

"This ain't over, motherfucker." He yelled out from the window.

"Come get some more. I'll beat your ass again. My

pleasure, motherfucker!" I yelled back.

I looked over at Tiffany, and we locked eyes for a minute as she started the car. I shook my head at her. She mouthed, "I'm sorry". Tiffany then quickly drove off.

I continued standing there, watching them drive off down the street. I couldn't believe this shit just happened! How did he know where I live? Was he stalking me? I shook it off and went back inside. I called Daniel and told him what went down, just in case it ever happened again. After an hour or so, I got off the phone with Daniel. I went into the kitchen and poured up a drink. I sat back in my recliner and finished watching Martin.

45 minutes later, I felt my phone vibrate and looked at it. It was a long text from Tiffany.

"I'm so sorry that happened Darryl. He went through my phone when I got home that day, and I guess he took it from there. I had no idea he was going to do that. I never wanted this to happen to you. To us. I knew my life was a mess. I should have stuck to my decision and stayed away from you. I am so sorry for all of the drama I have caused you and brought into your life. Please don't hate me. I hope you can find it in your heart to forgive me one day. I will stay away from you for good. Goodbye."

As much drama as she caused me, I didn't want her to leave me alone. I still wanted to be with her. I finally found someone that completed every aspect I was looking for. She made me happy. I responded in a moment of weakness.

"Tiffany don't do this. I love you, and I'm willing to make this work if you are. I'm willing to forget this all happened and start over."

"It's too much Darryl. It just wouldn't work. Please forgive me. Goodbye. For real this time."

I called her and she didn't answer the phone. I called again and she sent me to voicemail. I felt myself getting angry with her again. I went to her name in my contacts and stared at the block option for a while. But decided against it. Yet, I deleted her number and messages from my phone.

I was done playing this game with her. In that moment, I decided to let it go. I wasn't going to keep chasing a woman that didn't want to be chased.

The old D. Glove was surely going to make a comeback. I tried this love shit, and it's not for me. Too damn complicated.

Chapter 17

Tiffany

April 2019

"So, Calvin. You're having trouble with earning her trust back. And now Tiffany has begun seeing someone. Tiffany, can you explain to him why it's so hard for you to trust him again. And we will later address your infidelity." Our therapist stated.

"Calvin, this isn't the first, second, third or fourth time you have cheated on me. It's been multiple times. Why can't the man who committed his life to me just be faithful to me? We've been to therapy before. I kept my commitment to working through my emotions and trusting you again. But you broke your commitment and cheated on me again."

"You cheated on me too. I even got my ass beat for it."

"Calvin, my infidelity only came after you cheated on me multiple times. And I didn't tell you to start a fight with him."

"Calvin, you will get your chance to address Tiffany's infidelity. Tiffany, continue on." Our therapist chimed in. I continued.

"Calvin, I moved from my family to be with you. I moved to support you and prove to you that I was all in. I lost my relationship with my family defending you. I lost myself trying to be the perfect wife for you. Tried changing myself to be the woman you would love and never cheat on again. Only for you to cheat on me again. Tell me Calvin, what is it about her? What makes her so special; that you would drag me from Alabama to Texas; only to dump me like a rag doll?"

"Don't say that Tiff. Don't be so dramatic about it."

"Don't invalidate her feelings, Calvin. She is speaking her truth. Answer her question, please." Our therapist stated.

Calvin seemed to struggle to find the words to say.

"Be honest Calvin. I want the truth."

Calvin put his head down, but our therapist asked him to look me in the eye. He obliged.

"In 2015, I met her in Montgomery at one of the seminars held during the annual Southern News Conference. We were paired together for one of the speaking engagements workshops. She was in town from Houston. She was a senior in college and was going to graduate at the end of the year. She was starting an internship as a Meteorologist at the same station we currently work at, in January of the next year. Her grandfather had part ownership in the company; and she was following the family's legacy. The more we talked, I realized that she, that she- -"

Calvin stumbled over his words.

"Be honest with her, Calvin. That's what we are here for."

"I realized that she had star quality. She was exciting. She was fun. We were on the same level with what we wanted in life. You were content with being behind the scenes. I wanted you to want more for yourself. But you didn't. And she was striving for more. That attracted me to her. I swear, I was working on being faithful. I really tried. I told her I was married; but she didn't mind. We started seeing each other every day during and after the conference. Hooking up between sessions and when they dismissed us."

"Sorry to interrupt. But for my understanding, Calvin. How long is the conference?" Our therapist asked.

"A week." I answered for him, burning with rage on the inside.

"Okay, thanks. Continue on."

"On the last day of the conference, we went out for a farewell dinner. And that is when Tracy caught us, and got you involved. So, after things died down, I snuck out and went to her hotel room. She told me that she was really feeling me and hated that this had to end. I told her I didn't want it to end as well. She then informed me that Houston was having a position opening soon. Due to one of the anchors moving to New York for Good Morning America. She said if I was serious about her, she would talk to her grandfather about considering me for the position. I saw that as my ticket to a bigger market. That's why I took all of those trips to Houston. I had to secure my spot and prove to her grandfather that I was serious. And sure enough, I got the job in Houston. And here we are."

This bastard! He let a damn college student disrupt our marriage. The more details I found out; the more I regretted my decision to take him back. I felt so damn stupid!

"So, tell me how y'all got back together once we moved here."

Calvin dropped his head again.

"Eyes up, Calvin." Our therapist said to him.

"About two weeks after we got settled in Houston, I started seeing her again. By this time, she was close to finishing her internship at the station. We would see each other at the station, and away from the station."

"So that's why I was never invited to your job or any work functions? Because she was there? All those excuses about you not being able to have a plus one because you were new was a lie?"

"Yes." He said with a head nod.

"Go on."

"As time went on, she wanted more of my time. That's when I started disappearing more. Then things got more intense between us when you went back home to Montgomery. With her having me all to herself, she didn't want it to end. She wanted me to leave you at this point. And I felt that I had to in order to keep my job. This was around the time the station started preparing for Hurricane Harvey. Also, around this time, her internship ended. Hurricane Harvey would be her first time live on the news. We knew once you saw her, our cover would have been blown. So, we came up with a plan for my exit. I had a better way of presenting to you that I wanted a divorce, I swear I did. But when you got there and confronted me; all hell broke loose. I was caught off guard and reacted defensively."

"So, you chose a job over me? We could've just gone back to Montgomery."

Calvin had nothing to say.

"So, what changed your mind? Why did you come back for me now?"

"I jeopardized our relationship for something new, and I regret it. So, I broke it off. The more time I spent without you, I realized that being with you is where I belong. I do not want to throw away years of marriage for a fling. It took me months to realize that, but I realize it now and I am here to stay. I'm serious this time, Tiff. I want you, and I'll do anything to have you back. I'll do anything to make it right."

The room fell silent again until our therapist spoke up.

"How do you feel hearing Calvin's explanation?"

"I'm speechless. I always wanted the full story, and now I don't know what to say. It's hard to hear that he had a whole life planned with this woman."

Tears started to fall. My emotions were mixed between anger and hurt.

"Well on that note, we will conclude today's session. And we will pick up our next session talking about Tiffany's infidelity. For your homework assignment, I want you guys to do something fun today. You've had such a breakthrough moment this session. You need something to lighten the load. And for the next two weeks, I want you both to practice on the communication techniques we went over this morning. If you have any questions in between now and our next scheduled appointment, please do not hesitate to reach out to me. See you guys soon."

Calvin and I said our goodbyes and headed out. We decided our fun activity was to go out for lunch and drinks. Shortly after, we arrived at Pappadeaux's. As soon as we sat down, I asked for a Category 5. I needed something strong to settle my nerves from what I just heard.

Calvin had been hesitant to give me the full story on him and Tabitha. Today was the first time he had been completely forthcoming and transparent in the months we had been in counseling. I questioned if he was being fully honest, though. Him saying that he came back for me because he realized how much he loved me; was not sitting right with me. Something had to have happened. Something big. I could not put my finger on it just yet. But I was going to find out.

As we sipped our drinks and waited for our food, I noticed Calvin kept checking his phone.

"Damn, that phone sure is getting more attention than I am." I rolled my eyes and sipped on my drink.

"I'm sorry baby. They are having an issue at work and may need me to come in."

Soon after, he excused himself to make a call to his boss.

While alone, my mind drifted off to Darryl. I found myself thinking a lot about Darryl lately. What he was doing. How he has been. I even thought about him during sex with Calvin sometimes. He was so much better than Calvin. Darryl introduced me to new things and sexual pleasure I never knew existed. As I thought more and more about Darryl; Calvin made it back to the table without me noticing him. I must have dazed out. I came to, hearing Calvin calling my name.

"Tiffany! Tiffany! The food is here. Make room for your plate."

After lunch we went to a movie; then finally headed back to the house.

I went into the bathroom and took a shower. I kept

replaying our therapy session from earlier today. Things were so different between Calvin and I this time. I questioned everything about him. My thought was disturbed by a knock on the door.

"How long you going to be in there? I want to shower too."

"I'm sorry. I'll be out soon."

I finished up and got out of the shower. As I was drying myself off, Calvin walked in.

"I want to thank you for being so patient with me. I know I have been a terrible husband over the years. I plan to turn that all around. I want you to believe and trust me again. I'm vowing to earn it all back." Calvin said before he kissed me.

I smiled at him and then walked out. I went to the kitchen to pour myself a glass of wine. I then heard the shower turn on. I curled up on the couch with my glass of Cabernet. Once Calvin got out of the shower, he poured himself a glass of whiskey and sat in the recliner next to me. After a while, I went into the kitchen and popped a bag of popcorn. I grabbed both the wine and whiskey and brought it all into the living room with us. We continuously filled up our glasses as we watched television and ate popcorn; until we fell asleep.

I woke up at around 10PM to the television playing the theme song to Good Times. I took the bottles of wine and whiskey, and the bags of popcorn into the kitchen to throw away. I came back to the living room, and Calvin was still asleep. When he drinks, he goes into a deep slumber and it's a struggle to get him up. I managed to get him up though and walked him to the bedroom. I helped him into the bed, where he passed out. I took his phone out of his pocket and placed it on the nightstand. It lit up and I saw Tabitha's name come across the screen. She sent him a message an hour ago.

My heart started racing. I've always checked his phone but have recently been making it a habit to stop, since I would see so many things I didn't want to see. But I couldn't help myself this time. I poked at him to see if he would wake up. He didn't. I used his finger to unlock his phone. I then went into the bathroom and locked the door. I sat on the toilet and prepared myself for what I was about to see. The phone opened to his call log screen. He had been calling her all day! Since the time we left the therapy session, until the time we got home. And I found out he lied when he said that his boss was calling, because his boss' name was nowhere to be found in the call log. I went to the messages and clicked on her name. The messages only went back to late November.

Sent-November 19th, 2018- 5:28PM: I love you baby. I can be a better man. Give me another chance.

Sent- November 20th, 2018- 10:01AM: Does this mean we're not spending Thanksgiving together? I was excited to meet your family. ☹

Sent-November 22nd, 2018- 8:08AM: Happy Thanksgiving babe! 😊

Sent-November 24th, 2018- 11:22: Baby, I lost my cool. It will never happen again.

Received-November 24th, 2018- 12:13PM: We're done Calvin. You showed your ass for the last time. I can't take your controlling ways anymore. I told you he was just an old friend from college. You embarrassed me and yourself. Go back to your wife. Both of y'all tired asses deserve each other.

Sent-November 24th,2018-12:15PM: I was afraid I was losing you. I can admit I get nervous sometimes thinking you're going to leave me for a younger man. I can change. Let me make it up to you.

Sent-December 25th, 2018- 6:32PM: Merry Christmas! 😊 Wish I could have spent it with you. Yet I had to spend it alone. ☹ I still love you baby and think about you daily. Please just talk to me.

Sent-January 1st, 2019- 12:01AM: Happy New Year. New year, new beginnings.

Received-January 1st, 2019- 1:17PM: If you don't stop contacting me, I will have you fired from the station Calvin. I cannot continue working with you acting like this. I'm changing my shift tomorrow. Please get yourself some help.

Sent-February 14th, 2019- 2:48PM: Happy Valentine's

Day! Do you remember how much fun we had last year? Wish we could have made another year worth of memories. I miss you.

Sent-February 18th, 2019- 8:06PM: I don't need you, bitch. I am back with my wife where I'm appreciated. I am not going to keep chasing you! Have fun with that clown you are with. He can never be me. You will miss me when I'm gone!

Sent-March 22nd, 2019- 3:36PM: I'm so happy I got back with my wife. What was I thinking leaving her for a slut like you? Here's some pictures of us for you to see what you're missing!!!! *2 Attachments Sent*

Sent-April 10th, 2019- 1:48AM: Today I thought about you and I miss you baby. I tried making it work with my wife, but she's not you. I want you. I don't want to be with her. Please call me. We can work this out.

Received Today-April 26th, 2019- 9:17PM: Calvin, please stop contacting me! I told you it was over. I'm filing a restraining order against you Monday morning. It's been almost six months. MOVE ON! I HAVE MOVED ON WITH MY LIFE! I HOPE YOU CAN DO THE SAME! WE'RE DONE!

I placed the phone down on the sink and sat there for a moment. I was enraged! All this time, he was telling me one thing while still trying to get her back. I knew something was wrong. This bastard made *me* the rebound. I took him back and swallowed my pride. I left Darryl for him! And it was all for nothing. I took screen shots of the messages and came out of the bathroom. I saw him lying there. His mouth was wide open; snoring loud enough to wake the neighborhood.

I was disgusted with him. The way he begged and begged for her. Here I am looking like a fool, while he is out here looking like a bigger fool. How embarrassing! I balled my fist up and cocked back as far as I could. I had the thought of pouncing on him and kicking his ass but decided against it. I then thought about throwing his phone at him with all my might but decided against that too. I was better than this. No need for violence this time. I'll just leave. I placed his phone back on the nightstand. I quietly packed all my clothes and my belongings and put them by the door. I wrote him a note and left it next to his phone before leaving out.

"I read the messages between you and her. All of them. And don't try to lie about it. I sent the messages to myself. Have a nice life trying to win her back. I am done with you and your bullshit for the last time. I want a divorce!"

I left the house with rage in my heart. No more tears this time. I instantly thought to call Tracy. But since I got back with Calvin, I've been avoiding her out of shame. So, I called Lauren.

"Lauren, can you meet me please?"

"Where are you? Are you okay?"

"I left the house and am on my way to my apartment. I'll tell you everything when you get here. Use your key. And please bring the strongest drink you have on you."

"Okay girl, on my way."

I hung up the phone and soon arrived at my apartment. Thank God I didn't get rid of this apartment; or I would've been calling Lauren for a place to stay. Again.

I left everything in the car and went inside. I went straight to the kitchen. I looked around for any liquor; hoping I left some here. But I must have finished it all. I sat down at the kitchen table and put my head down. I felt a headache brewing.

How could I be so stupid! Rage came over me again. I had Tabitha's number from Calvin's phone. I wanted to call her and curse her out. As soon as I went looking for her number, I heard keys rattling in the door. Lauren walked in, and I put the phone down. She called out my name. I did not respond. She kept calling out for me until she walked in and saw me sitting at the table.

"Tiffany, hon. What's wrong. You're scaring me."

"I gave that bastard 15 years of my life. Gave him my virginity. Miscarried 3 times from stress trying to have his baby. Isolated and estranged myself from my family. Moved across the South following behind him. And this bastard still cheating on me. With the same bitch. I'm the dummy! I'm the fool!"

Lauren came up to me and hugged me.

"Don't beat yourself up, friend."

Lauren went into the kitchen and pulled out some glasses. She poured us up two shots and handed it to me.

"How did you find out?"

I took my shot and went over the story with Lauren. I also showed her the screenshots I took from his phone.

"That dirty devil. Disrupted your life because he got rejected. And the nerve of him to be so thirsty and begging her like that. Pathetic!"

I shook my head in disgust.

"To see him beg for her really disgusted me. How desperate!"

I poured myself another shot.

"What are you going to do friend?"

I rubbed my head and came up with the only possible solution.

"I'm filing for a divorce, bright and early Monday morning. And I'm going to get my man back."

Chapter 18

Tiffany

June 2019

"**D**rinks up, bitches!!! Let's get this party started!!!! My friend is divorced and belongs to the streets tonight!"

Two months had passed, and my divorce was finalized yesterday morning! Me, Lauren, and several of our workout buddies were on a party bus, headed to a few spots downtown. I thought about inviting Jalisa but wasn't sure yet how I was going to explain this to Darryl. And I know if Jalisa knew, she was going to tell Daniel, who was going to tell Darryl.

Calvin initially tried to give me push back with the divorce; but after mediation, he backed down. I could've taken his ass through the ringer financially, but I settled for a lumpsum of $15,000. A stack for each year spent with his trifling ass. My time and commitment were worth more than that. But I didn't want to drag the process out any longer than it needed to be. I was free. Happy, paid and free!

"Pour me another shot Lauren!" I shouted over the music.

After drinking and partying the night away, the night ended with me at Lauren's place. Lauren wanted to have a sleep over "after party", so I packed an overnight bag. I sat in the living room while Lauren showered. When she came out, I went in and showered.

After getting out the shower and getting dressed, we sat on her bed and started watching television. I took a moment to reflect on life and my journey. Two years ago, I was here *suffering* the breakup of my marriage. Tonight, I was here *celebrating* the breakup of my marriage. Ironic, right? Amazing how life can change in two years.

"So, what is going on with Darryl? Are you finally going to reach out to him now that you're officially divorced?" She said sluggishly from all the drinking and partying.

"I was so confident initially, but after thinking things over; I just don't know. I've caused so much damage and hurt. Sometimes I wonder if he will even take me back. Especially after the fight they had. I've been calling him continuously since, and he hasn't returned my calls. I even called him for his birthday and didn't get a response. What should I do?"

"Tiffany, I'm going to be frank with you. You finally get

rid of Calvin, and don't know what you should do? Come on now, friend. Why come this far and give up on Darryl? That man loved you and did whatever it took to get you. If you have to bend over backwards trying to win him back; that's what you will need to do. Do not let a good one pass you by. You worked hard at keeping a no-good man; I think you can work hard at keeping a good one."

"But what if he's back with that older woman I saw him with? He ran straight to her last time; and I'm pretty sure he did it again."

"You said so yourself that he was angry and hurt. She's probably just a rebound. You know men. They need to have their egos stroked. He probably only with her for a good time after being hurt by you. Whatever he's doing, you cannot hold that against him. Either you be his woman, or you let someone else be. It's as simple as that."

Lauren's words smacked me in the face, but she was right. If I really wanted Darryl, I was going to have to go and get him. And my, my, my! I *really* wanted him. I couldn't stop thinking about him. I looked up to respond, and Lauren was drifting off to sleep. I could see all those shots had gotten to her. I quietly giggled because Lauren was more drunk than me, and it was my divorce party. I tucked her in the bed and turned off the tv. I grabbed my phone, quietly closed the door, and went into the living room.

I sat down on the couch and sipped on a bottle of water, trying to sober up.

Lauren was right. I pushed Darryl into that woman's arms. I had no right to feel some kind of way. I tossed my phone back and forth. Toying with the idea of calling him.

It had been months since I have seen Darryl. I managed to dodge him at the office and other work gatherings. I listened to him every night on the radio, though. Some nights I even pleasured myself to the sound of his voice. That voice, ooh that voice. It just did something to me. And the voice was only the beginning. His body, his hands, his delicious chocolate skin, those white teeth! Goddamn, that man is fine! Sitting here thinking about him got me hot with passion. I soon found myself ordering an Uber to Darryl's house. I had to see him!

Driver: Hampton Thomas

Color/Make/Model/: White Toyota Camry

License Plate: RBC 6239

Arrival Time: 3 Minutes

My Uber soon arrived, and I grabbed the overnight bag I packed for the sleepover. I checked in on Lauren and she was knocked out. I sent a simple text to her before walking out the door.

"I'm going to get my man."

I then left out of the house quietly. My Uber driver was an older black man. I looked at the name again. 'Hampton

Thomas'. This name seemed familiar. I got in the backseat of the car and put on my seat belt.

"You okay, gal? Pretty late for you to be out in these streets."

"Yes, sir. I'm fine. I was going to ask you the same thing. I'm surprised you're out driving around this time of night."

"I've seen so many young people die due to drunk driving. I'm just doing my part in making sure you young folks get to be as old as me. And since I have retired, I need something to keep me going. You're actually my last ride of the night."

I looked out of the window as we trailed to Darryl's home.

"If you don't mind me asking; where are you going this late baby girl?"

"An ex of mine. I really screwed things up with him, and I'm hoping I could make it right tonight. I didn't even call him to make sure he was up. I'm winging it, sir."

I could not believe I was telling this old man all of my business. That liquor was really working on me.

"He must be really special, to have you out here this late at night."

I smiled to myself.

"Yes, sir. He is."

"I wish you the best of luck, baby girl."

"Thank you, sir."

We soon arrived at Darryl's place.

"This is it?"

"Yes sir."

"Wait a minute. I know this house. This is Darryl's home. Your ex is Darryl Glover?"

How did he know Darryl? I looked at the name again. Then it all clicked. He was Mr. Thomas; the guy I replaced at the radio station.

"Oh my god, you're Mr. Thomas! Darryl told me so much about you. I'm Tiffany. The engineer who took over your shift at the radio station."

Mr. Thomas parked the car and turned around.

"You don't say! So, you are the woman who changed his life. He's also told me so much about you."

"So, you think I have a chance at winning him back?"

"You have more than chance. You have love. Go get that boy and put him out of his misery. And don't tell him you met me. I'll call that knucklehead tomorrow."

"Thank you so much, Mr. Thomas."

"Sure. Now go on. I'll wait here until I see you are inside."

I got out of the car and walked to the door. I looked at the time. 2:24AM. I knocked on the door and waited. I rang the doorbell and knocked some more. Then I heard him walking towards the door.

"Who is it?"

"It's me, Tiffany."

Darryl opened the door.

"What are you doing here?"

I opened my mouth to respond but was caught off guard by Mr. Thomas honking his horn twice. I turned around and Mr. Thomas was driving off.

"Tiffany, what are you doing here? It's 2:30 in the morning."

"Can I come in, please?"

Darryl stepped aside, and I walked in. I sat my bag on the steps.

"Tiffany, what do you want? Why are you here?"

"I came here to talk."

"About what? What do you want to talk about Tiffany?"

Ooh, I could tell he was up-set.

"About us Darryl."

"Everything is always on your terms, huh? I guess when it's convenient for you, you're ready to pick me back up? That's how it's going down, right?"

"I know I was wrong Darryl. For everything. I was wrong. From leaving you in the beginning, to coming back here confusing you, to the fight between y'all two. I caused all of that, and I'm sorry. I genuinely apologize. I want to make things right. And I hope that you can find it in your heart to forgive me and take me back."

I walked over to Darryl and started kissing him. Then I started tugging at his pants.

"No. *NO!* Stop Tiffany!"

Darryl grabbed my hands and pushed me off him.

"You don't get the pleasure of waltzing in here like nothing is wrong. You have some explaining to do! What is up with you?"

"I fucked up Darryl, okay? I was wrong about my husband. I shouldn't have gone back to him. I screwed up what you and I had for a man that had no intentions of doing right by me. I was a fool, but I promise I won't be a fool again."

"So, I'm the rebound guy? That clown showed his ass for what? The hundredth time now? And you finally decide to get some sense and leave him? And you think you are going to come back to me after he done used you up? Fuck that, Tiffany. And nah, *I* was a fool to think I could make you love me. And *I* will not be a fool again. Now please leave."

His words cut me deep. But I wasn't giving up. I knew he was talking from a place of hurt and not from his heart.

"I'm not leaving until we work this out."

I knew he wanted me as bad as I needed him right now. I walked up to him and tried kissing him again. He stopped me and backed off.

"Stop fighting me, Darryl. You know you want it as bad

as I do. I know you miss me. I miss you too, baby. Can you forgive me? *Please?* I promise I won't hurt you anymore. Just give me a chance to make it right. I love you. I love you so much."

I kissed him again. He tried pushing away, but I pressed my body into his. Ignoring his attempt to fight me off. He finally gave in and kissed me back. Seems like instantly we started snatching off each other's clothes. He backed up and we stared at one another. We were both standing there naked, breathing rugged; admiring one another's body. He picked me up and I straddled him. He was rock hard, and I could feel him against me. He walked over to the dining room table and sat down in a chair. I straddled him and quickly inserted him inside of me.

Feeling him inside of me again was a slice of heaven. As he guided my body up and down, up and down; I stared into his eyes with satisfaction and desire. He then laid his head back and his eyes rolled to the back of his head. A moan escaped his lips. He bit his bottom lip and enjoyed the ride. I kept my rhythm and control over him. I wanted him to know how much my body missed him. How much my body yearned for him.

"I'm so sorry baby. I swear, I am done with him for good. I divorced him. I'm all yours now if you'll have me."

That broke his trance, and his eyes zoned in on me. He

jumped up, walked us over to the sofa and put me down. I started to move the pillows from under me, but he snatched them and threw them across the room. He kneeled down and slid into me. Then, he started pounding on me. Really hard. It was pain and pleasure all wrapped into one.

"I waited for you. For months. Hoping you would come back to me. But you didn't."

"I'm. Sorry. Baby." I said with each stroke as he continued pounding inside of me.

His thrusts became harder.

"You played me. You hurt my feelings. And now you come crawling back. I bet he don't fuck you like I do. Daddy good to you? You miss it, don't you? You miss Daddy?"

I didn't respond; I was so far gone in my own zone.

"I said! You. Miss. It. Don't. You?" He said with each thrust.

The serious tone of his voice snapped me back to reality. He grabbed my thighs, lifted me partially, and drilled into me. I quickly looked up at him and his eyes seems as if they were piercing into my soul.

"Yes baby! I miss it! I miss you! I promise I will never leave you again!"

"You damn right. Don't you ever leave me again!"

Oh God. I felt erotica rising and building up inside of me as Darryl kept his rhythm, hitting my spot.

"Darryl, baby. I'm. About. To. Cum!!!!"

My body erupted with pleasure. I felt Darryl pulsating and releasing inside of me. I missed that feeling of him filling me up.

Both of us were breathing out of control, sweaty and staring at one another. I broke the silence.

"I love you, Darryl."

"I love you too, Tiffany."

I had my man back.

Chapter 19

Darryl

September 2019

"Happy birthday to you. Happy birthday to you. Happy birthday dear Tiffany. Happy birthday to you!"

We all sung the Happy Birthday song to Tiffany. Me, Tiffany, Lauren, Daniel, and Jalisa were on a 5-day vacation trip to the Bahamas for Tiffany's birthday. Tiffany wanted sun in the Caribbean, so I gave her just that. She said she wanted sunshine because that's how she was feeling at the time. And I couldn't agree more. I had the woman of my dreams all to myself; as she had me. No more Calvin, the estranged husband. And no more Carmen, the friend with benefits. We were all in this time around. All strings attached.

We were out having dinner at a restaurant on the beach. It was the first day of our vacation and I had a lot of things planned. We were enjoying seafood and cocktails when Daniel started clinking his fork on the glass.

"I have an announcement I'd like to make. As we welcome Tiffany back into the family; Jalisa and I will be bringing an addition to this family as well. As some of you may know, Jalisa and I have had some pregnancy complications. But we finally did it. My baby is having a baby, y'all! She's four months pregnant."

Jalisa then took off her covering and showed off her growing belly. I jumped up with excitement.

"Are you serious, bro? I'm going to be an uncle?"

"Yep, you sure are."

"I can't believe y'all hid this from me!"

"Yea, we wanted to be sure this time before we made any announcements."

"Let me see that belly!"

I went over to Jalisa and rubbed her belly. My niece or nephew is in there! I then walked over to Daniel and gave him a hug.

"Congratulations, Daniel. I can't express how happy I am for you."

"Thanks, *Uncle Darryl.*"

I heard footsteps in high heels approaching our table.

"What's all the excitement about? I know y'all didn't start the party without me!"

Tiffany immediately turned around.

"Oh my God!" Tiffany started to cry.

She turned back and looked at me with confusion. Then turned back around. It was as if she seen a ghost.

"Tracy, what are you doing here?"

"Well don't just stand there. Give your sister a hug. Darryl didn't fly me out here just for you to stare at me."

Tiffany got up and gave Tracy a hug with the biggest smile on her face. Tiffany looked at me.

"You got her here? How? When? You planned all of this?"

"I sure did." I said with a smirk.

Tracy chimed in. "Yep, he's the one who arranged for me to be here. Paid for my trip and all. After missing your birthday, a couple times, I couldn't miss it again."

Tiffany turned back to me.

"Thank you, baby. You have truly given me a wonderful birthday, again. You never cease to amaze me. I love you!"

She leaned over and kissed me.

"Love you too, babe. And remember, it's only Day 1 of our trip. We got four more days to go. Just wait to see what I have in store next."

Tiffany's face lit up with excitement. I loved seeing her happy.

"Everyone, this is Tracy. My big sister." Tiffany walked

over to Tracy and hugged her again. "I'm so happy you're here." She said in between sniffles.

"I'm happy to be here, sis."

Tiffany walked Tracy around, introducing her to everyone else. She then wiped her face.

"Enough of these tears. Let's go get some footage of Jalisa and this belly!" Tiffany said as she rubbed Jalisa's belly.

Tiffany, Tracy, Lauren and Jalisa walked off, laughing and talking. They found a spot with a good view and started taking pictures of Jalisa and her baby bump.

I walked over to Daniel and handed him a beer. I put mines on the table next to his.

"Congratulations again, big brother. You guys have been trying so hard to have a baby. I'm glad it's finally happening."

"Yea, the doctor confirmed yesterday that we made it to the second trimester, and she should finally carry full term this time."

"That's wonderful."

"The Glover brothers strike again, huh? You have finally met the woman of your dreams; and I'm going to be a father soon. This is what it's all about. Love and happiness. How soon until I'm your best man?" Daniel joked.

"Hold on, now. You're moving too fast. Let's focus on buying diapers before you go buying a tux."

We laughed.

"But for real, Darryl. I'm happy for you. I'm happy for us. What a time to be alive, right?"

"Right."

We extended a cheers to each other and watched our women in the sunset.

I admired looking at Tiffany while she laughed with the girls. She was glowing. You could see the joy radiating from her. I wouldn't be surprised if somebody said I was glowing also. I was happy to have Tiffany. I was a lucky man.

I reminisced on how I never thought I could fall in love. I guess it just took the right woman to change all of that for me. In my 36 years of living, I never felt as strongly for someone as I did in these past 2 years. Tiffany definitely shook up my world and made life more meaningful. I sipped my beer and watched the love of my life enjoy life.

Life is complete. Life is set. Life is good.

About the Author

Kella was born and raised in New Orleans, Louisiana. In 10th grade, sitting in class at McDonogh 35 Senior High School, Kella began writing short stories to pass time. Her stories began being passed around school to her friends, who overwhelmed her with their great feedback. Sadly, during her Senior Year of High School, Hurricane Katrina uprooted Kella and life as she knew it. In addition, her short stories and passion for writing were also destroyed. Fortunately: many years later, Kella found her passion again for writing, and started back up again.

Kella is a writer of black, romance novels. She enjoys telling stories from all aspects of the black community, and their relationships.

www.ingramcontent.com/pod-product-compliance
Lightning Source LLC
Chambersburg PA
CBHW021152110726
47900CB00002B/535